Claudia and the Disaster Date

Other books by
Ann M. Martin

Claudia and the
Disaster Date

Ann M. Martin

AN
APPLE
PAPERBACK

SCHOLASTIC INC.
New York   Toronto   London   Auckland   Sydney
Mexico City   New Delhi   Hong Kong

No part of this publication may be reproduced in whole or in part, or stored in a retrieval system or transmitted in any form or by any means, electronic, mechanical, photocopying, recording, or otherwise, without written permission of the publisher. For information regarding permission, write to Scholastic Inc., Attention: Permissions Department, 555 Broadway, New York, NY 10012.

ISBN 0-590-52348-1

12 11 10 9 8 7 6 5 4 3 2 1   0/0 1 2 3 4 5/0

Printed in the U.S.A.   40

First Scholastic printing, October 2000

*The author gratefully acknowledges
Nola Thacker
for her help in
preparing this manuscript.*

Claudia and the Disaster Date

❋ Chapter 1

Dancing with a guy is not the same as going out on an actual date with him.

Especially when the guy is Alan Gray.

I glanced at him, half expecting to see fake green slime oozing out of his nose or something. But his nose was slime-free, to my relief.

"Popcorn?" Alan asked. "I could buy some and you could go pick out seats."

I hesitated. Could I trust Alan to get popcorn that was, well, just popcorn?

Stop it, I scolded myself. This Alan Gray was not the cornball-jokes, gross-out-humor Alan Gray. This was a different Alan.

The real Alan. Whoever that was.

"Okay," I said.

"Butter?" he asked.

I wrinkled my nose. "I'm not really crazy about movie-theater butter," I told him. "It's kind of yucky sometimes."

"Like slime," Alan said, as if he'd read my thoughts. I felt my cheeks grow warm, but fortunately Alan didn't notice. "Just salt, then. And sodas."

"Real soda," I said. "No diet junk."

"A girl who appreciates genuine junk food. I like that," said Alan.

My cheeks grew warmer still. Alan couldn't know it, but he spoke the truth. Beneath my artistically pulled-together exterior was the soul — or stomach — of a junk food fiend.

There was a lot Alan and I didn't know about each other, a lot we had to learn.

Dates were supposed to fix that. You went on a date and learned about the person behind the artistic (or gross-out) exterior and decided whether you really liked or really couldn't stand the real deal.

"Claudia? Earth to Claudia . . ." Alan waved his hand.

"Oh. Sorry." I smiled. "Two seats, center aisle, coming up." I crossed the lobby of the Stoneybrook Cinema, glancing nervously around. It wasn't just first-date, going-out-with-Alan-Gray nerves. It was first-date, going-out-with-Alan-Gray-*secretly* nerves.

I hadn't told anyone about my Monday afternoon plans. Not my fellow members of the Baby-sitters Club (or BSC), not even my best friend, Stacey McGill. If the date went well, I reasoned, I'd tell everyone at the BSC meeting later that afternoon. If not, well, what people didn't know wouldn't hurt them.

Or me.

Or Alan.

I made it into the nice, semidark theater without seeing anyone I knew. There were two empty seats just where I like to sit. I took one and put my sweater on the one next to me. Even though it was July, I knew that before the movie was over, I'd need it. The Stoneybrook Cinema is freezing in the summer and stuffy as an oven in the winter.

I slid down and began to relax just a little. Memories of dancing with Alan came back to me. Alan had been sweet and a little awkward, clearly on his best behavior and not at all like the Alan Gray that my friends and I knew and avoided.

My mind went further back. I've lived in Stoneybrook all my life and I've known Alan since first grade — Alan the Gross: Alan burping on pitch to "Row, Row, Row Your Boat"; Alan with yellow

M&M's squinted between scrunched-up eyes at Mary Anne's surprise Halloween party, announcing that he was Little Orphan Annie; Alan bursting out of the boys' bathroom seconds before a cherry bomb exploded with a truly impressive BOOM. (He got suspended for that one.)

How could I go out with a boy who had a past like that? How could he and I have any kind of future? I mean, it's not that I'm perfect or anything. Ask my work-hard parents or my genius older sister, Janine. They don't understand my artistic vision of the world any more than I understand how they can find any satisfaction in doing their taxes (and math homework, in Janine's case).

"Pardon me, but is this seat taken?"

"Alan!" I exclaimed, straightening in my seat.

He looked surprised. "Yeah, it's me. You were expecting maybe . . ." I could almost see him thinking about making a cornball joke.

"You," I said hastily. I yanked my sweater away and motioned for him to sit down. "Are these seats okay?"

"Great." He carefully put my soda into the cup holder, handed me the popcorn and napkins, and sat down.

"You remembered napkins," I said. When it

comes to movie-theater popcorn, buttered *or* un, napkins are crucial to the survival of whatever you're wearing. But not everyone agrees with me. Lots of guys and at least one girl — our fearless BSC president, Kristy Thomas — believe that jeans can double as napkins.

"For you, anything," said Alan, and laughed a little to show he was joking. He pulled a straw from his jacket pocket, carefully unwrapped it, and slid it into the drink.

I was touched. I admit it. Corny jokes don't move me, but small, corny, thoughtful gestures are a different story.

The lights in the theater dimmed. The endless advertisements began to roll. Since we were practically the only people in the theater and since no one was sitting near us, we felt free to ignore the less-than-subtle attempts to sell us all kinds of junk.

"I can't believe you haven't seen *The Tsunami Monster's Revenge*," Alan said. "It's a great movie, even if it's a cartoon."

"I've been wanting to see it," I confessed. "But I couldn't convince any of my friends to go. I love animated films. I mean, the good ones are real works of art. But my friends just don't understand."

"The bad ones are the worst, though," Alan said.

"Like those really crummy cartoons that used to be on Saturday morning television, with the characters moving like robots or something."

"It's true," I agreed. "Totally lame."

"Are you interested in animation?" Alan asked.

"Sure," I said. "But I don't think I'd be very good at it, even with the help of a computer."

"I wouldn't mind being a cartoonist. I'd like to have a comic strip. That would be fun. And I *do* have a great sense of humor."

I glanced at Alan, unsure whether he was being serious.

The movie started. I looked at the screen and looked back at Alan. He grinned at me, and I still wasn't sure if he was joking.

But then, I have never appreciated Alan's sense of humor. I wondered if I ever would.

Alan reached out. Oh, no! Was he going to try to hold my hand for the whole movie? I wasn't sure I was ready to hold hands for that long with Alan Gray, the new or the old version.

Then I realized that he was offering me the popcorn. Mortified (and glad he couldn't read my thoughts), I whispered, "Thanks." I shoved a handful of popcorn in my mouth, slid back down in my seat, and forced myself to concentrate on the screen.

After the movie, as we walked out of the theater, Alan cleared his throat and his shoulder bumped against mine. "So," he said. "Want to get something to eat? We could go to the Rosebud Café."

"It's tempting," I said, and I meant it. Mere popcorn and soda at a movie only stokes my junk food craving. "But I have to get to the Baby-sitters Club meeting. It's at my house, and people notice right away if I'm late."

I didn't mention that I also didn't want to have to endure the steely-eyed glare of Kristy if I arrived even a nanosecond after five-thirty, or to have to explain where I'd been and why I was late. Also, going to the Rosebud Café meant spending more time in public with Alan, which meant that someone might see us. I wasn't sure I was prepared for that either.

"I could walk you," Alan offered.

"No!" I said. "I mean, no, thanks. It's way out of your way."

Seeing Alan's crestfallen look, I added quickly, "I had a good time, Alan. I, uh, I . . . this was fun. I like hanging out with you, especially when you're not, you know, goofing around like you do at school. I mean, I'm not trying to insult you."

Alan gave me a grin with more than a trace of his old cocky smirk in it. "Don't worry," he said. "As long as you are saying we can do this again some-time. We don't even have to go to a movie. We could watch a softball game. Or go Rollerblading."

"I'd like that," I said. I glanced down at my watch. "Uh-oh. I've got to run. See ya!"

"Later," said Alan, trying to sound supersophisti-cated and almost succeeding.

I waved and raced off, not looking supersophisti-cated at all. As I dashed around the corner, I glanced back.

Alan was still standing there, grinning. Who was watching me dash away — the old Alan, or the new one?

I didn't have time to think about it. I made a face, dodged around the corner, and booked it for my house.

❋ Chapter 2

I blasted through the door of my own room and found the usual suspects: Dawn Schafer, back from California — where she lives with her father and his family — to spend the summer with her mother, Mary Anne Spier (her stepsister), and Mary Anne's father; Mary Anne; Kristy; and Stacey.

"Ahem." Kristy cleared her throat and looked pointedly at her watch.

"I'm not late," I said. "The clock on my desk says five-thirty exactly."

At that moment, the numbers rolled over to 5:31.

Kristy intoned, "This meeting of the BSC will now come to order," and it did.

I fell across the bed. "Whew."

"Where've you been?" asked Kristy, being her typical blunt self.

"Lost in the dark," I said lightly, sitting up. It was true. I'd been in a dark movie theater, totally lost in the film.

"It's summertime. It won't be dark until about nine," Kristy said.

"What happened to *you*?" I said, cleverly changing the subject. Kristy was wearing shorts and a T-shirt, as well as a large Band-Aid on one knee, a smaller one on her elbow, and quite a bit of dirt down one side of her body.

"A slide at home plate," she said impatiently.

"What?"

"Kristy was at the park, playing pickup softball with some of the girls from the SMS team," Mary Anne explained.

"Oh. Did you win?"

"I beat the throw at the plate," Kristy said. "But the other team won, more or less."

"More or less?" I was keeping Kristy from asking more questions by peppering her with questions myself.

"It was a friendly game. We weren't really keeping score." She paused, then couldn't help adding, "But my team was rallying when we left."

Before Kristy could resume her cross-examination of me, I bounced over to my closet, opened it, and pulled out my winter boots from the back. In the left one, I found a bag of candy corn. From the right one, I extracted a small can of mixed nuts and a bag of cheese-filled pretzels. I handed the mixed nuts to Kristy to open and forked the cheese pretzels over to Stacey, who is diabetic and can't eat much sugar.

Ripping open the candy corn, I popped a few in my mouth. Then I stuck two of them onto two upper teeth and leered. "Dracula," I said. "Get it?"

"That is *so* Alan Gray," Kristy said, catching me by surprise.

"What do you mean by that?" I demanded. I wondered if I was blushing.

"Only he'd probably have put them up his nose, not all that long ago," Mary Anne said. She smiled at me. "Don't you remember the time he got a fireball stuck in his nose in second grade? His father had to come get him and take him to the doctor to get it out. Alan was screaming like crazy."

"The fireball of snot," said Kristy, smiling at the memory.

I didn't smile. I decided just to ignore it. Maybe if I did, people would begin to forget about Alan's besmirched past and focus more on the new, improved version. I mean, everybody had noticed that he wasn't his old self these days.

Dawn and Stacey were both laughing. "I wish I'd moved to Stoneybrook sooner," Stacey said.

"Are you sure about that?" Dawn asked. She picked up a pretzel nugget, examined it suspiciously, then bit into it. Her expression said it was okay, but not great. Dawn is not a junk food fan, even of "healthy" junk food like pretzels.

The phone rang and caught us all by surprise. In the summer, especially in July, business is slow. Most of our clients are away on vacation or the kids are at camp.

Kristy fielded the call, then Mary Anne pulled out the appointment book and noted the sitting arrangements. After calling the clients back, Kristy hung up the phone and said, "So why were you almost late to the meeting, Claudia?"

"Well," I said, thinking fast, "I'm going to be working at the library. Starting tomorrow."

This didn't answer Kristy's question, but it distracted the BSC prez and everyone else. I was pleased with my skills of evasion.

"A real job?" Mary Anne said.

"For pay. Erica Blumberg and I are going to be

helping Ms. Feld in the kids' room." My mom is the head librarian at the Stoneybrook Public Library, but Erica and I had gotten the job fair and square through Ms. Feld.

"Decent," said Dawn.

Mary Anne smiled and said, "Are mysteries included?"

I smiled back. "I don't know, but you never can tell." Mary Anne was referring to the time she worked as a volunteer in the children's room and got all of us involved in solving a mystery there. A very hot mystery.

I went on. "Anyway, you remember Miss Ellway?"

"Of course," said Mary Anne. "The assistant children's librarian."

"Well, Mom promoted her, so she doesn't work in the children's room anymore. Until Ms. Feld hires a new assistant, Erica and I are going to fill in."

"Sounds like fun," Kristy commented. "And the children's room has story hours, right? So this is your chance to really boost their entertainment value, make it more than blah, blah, blah, show the illustration, turn the page. I mean, think of the props you can make, Claudia. Or you could get little kids to help you make the props for the stories. It's a perfect combination of your artistic talents and baby-sitting skills. Have you spoken to your mother about funding art supplies?"

I had to laugh and I wasn't the only one. Kristy was in her take-charge mode. "I've thought about that," I said. "But I haven't had a chance to talk to Mom. I'm going to call Erica tonight to do some brainstorming, and then after I see how things are set up, I'll bring it up with Ms. Feld or my mom."

Not only is my mom the head librarian, she's an *extreme* bibliophile, a word that means "she loves books." And boy, does she ever. But not just any books — what *she* calls good books.

My favorite books — anything Nancy Drew — do not count as good books in my mother's opinion. I keep a couple on my shelves with my other books, but I stash the rest along with my junk food and only indulge when my mother won't notice.

The Nancy Drew section at the library was, in my humble opinion, pretty limited. But I had a job there now and the rest of the summer to work on the situation.

"It's a great idea," Stacey said.

"We could help, if you ever need it," Dawn said. "I have a very free schedule and I think Mary Anne does too."

She glanced at Mary Anne, who nodded.

"Count me in," Kristy added.

"I'll count you all in," I promised.

We fielded one more phone call, then gossiped about this and that (Alan's name did not come up, to my relief). Soon it was time to go. Kristy adjourned the meeting, and she, Mary Anne, and Dawn strolled out.

Stacey stayed in her place on my bed. She kept her eyes on me as I tidied up a little, shoving a book into place on the bookshelf, putting a rubber band around the top of the candy corn before returning it to its hiding place.

"More pretzels?" I offered.

She shook her head, not blinking, not speaking. I cinched up the pretzels and put them away. I put what was left of the mixed nuts in the drawer of my bedside table, in case I was overcome with malnutrition in the middle of the night.

Stacey still hadn't spoken. She was getting on my last nerve.

"What?" I demanded. *"What?"*

"So where were you this afternoon?"

I took a deep breath. "Okay, okay, I confess," I said. "I was out on a . . . date."

I said the last word very softly.

Stacey sat upright. "Did you say *date*? With *who*? Why didn't you tell me?"

I answered the last two questions with two words: "Alan Gray."

"Alan Gray? Fireball-snot Alan Gray? *Again?*"

"That was second grade," I said. "I'm sure you weren't perfect in second grade either."

Stacey gave a little gasp of laughter and said, "True. I'll tell you a secret — it wasn't a fireball and it wasn't my nose."

"What — "

"It was gum. In my ear. I was trying to make earplugs." She shook her head. "I had to get most of my hair cut off. And it was about two days before the class picture. You should see it."

It was my turn to laugh. "Sounds like you were a fashion victim."

"It wasn't my best look," Stacey agreed wryly.

We were quiet for a minute. Then Stacey said, "You know, Claud, if you want to go out with Alan, he really must have changed."

"He has," I said. "He's thoughtful and considerate and . . . and he never makes those corny jokes. At least, he didn't today."

I went on to tell her about the big, secret date. "I just couldn't tell all of you, all at once," I concluded.

"It was too hard. I couldn't have stood Kristy's teasing."

"Teasing? That's putting it mildly," Stacey said. "If you start going out with Alan, it's going to be hard for Kristy and a few other people at SMS to take. They're still shocked that you *danced* with him in public."

"I know." I sighed. "I'll figure out something."

"You will," Stacey said.

I felt reassured, but not entirely. Going out with Alan seemed very complicated. Was he worth it?

❀ Chapter 3

When your mother is in charge of the library, you get to go in early on your first day of work. (Well, actually, you don't have a choice.) Mom and I arrived at the Stoneybrook Public Library at eight forty-five, an hour and fifteen minutes before the doors officially opened.

We weren't the only ones who were early. Erica was just locking her bike to the rack at one side of the door.

"Yo," I said to Erica, mimicking the character from the old movie *Rocky*.

"Hey," Erica replied. She and I have only recently become friends. I was glad we were going to work together this summer.

My mother nodded approvingly. "You're early, Erica."

"You're never late when you're early," Erica replied.

"That sounds like something a parental unit would say," I commented.

Erica grinned. "My father. He keeps all the clocks in the house fast. And there are a lot of clocks, believe me."

The door swung open and Mom motioned us inside. We followed her as she flicked on the lights. As we passed the mural in the hall leading to the children's room, I said, "Wow. It's starting to look kind of faded. I could give it a touch-up in no time. And maybe bring it up to speed. I mean, it *is* a little dated, you know?"

My mother said, "It's nice of you to offer to help. But your job is in the kids' room, helping Ms. Feld."

Behind my mother's back, I made a face at Erica. *Parents,* I mouthed.

"Maybe in my free time," I offered.

"You won't have much of that, if I know Dolores Feld," Mom commented.

As if on cue, Ms. Feld burst through the front door. "I'm here," she sang out, in what was *not* a quiet, library voice. "Oh, good, you girls are too. Give me half a minute to get organized . . . and get some coffee."

"I was just about to ask Claudia to show Erica where the break room is and how to put the coffeepot on," my mother said.

"Oh, good." Ms. Feld beamed at us. "Until I have a cup of coffee in the morning, I'm practically sleepwalking."

"This way," I said to Erica. The blast of Ms. Feld's energy was making me feel slow and tired.

When we were safely in the break room, which was hardly more than a long, narrow cubicle with a high, narrow horizontal window in the back of the library basement, Erica said, "Whoa. If she calls that sleepwalking, I'd hate to see it when she's awake."

I laughed. "Tell me about it. You'll get used to it, though. The kids love her."

Working carefully in the tiny, cluttered room (which, in addition to a table with a small refrigerator beneath it, a sink with two cabinets on the wall above it, and a lumpy sofa with a folding chair at either end, also contained a bookcase — as if there weren't enough already in the library!), we made coffee. It was just dripping into the pot when Ms. Feld stuck her head through the door, her brown curls springing up every which way on her head.

"Oh, *good*," she said. Her curls bobbed emphatically. Although Ms. Feld is a small woman, the break room suddenly seemed much more crowded. Reaching into the cabinet for a cup, Ms. Feld said at top speed, "We'll take it sort of slow today, let you learn the ropes. The morning reading group is a read-aloud for very young children. Short attention spans. Lots of forgetting to listen. Some parents drop them off and go to the adult section for that half hour, so it's important to keep the door closed and not let any of the little darlings wander away. Tears. I keep plenty of tissues at my desk, don't worry."

As she talked, Ms. Feld snatched the coffeepot from beneath the stream of coffee and shoved her cup under. Coffee hit the hot plate beneath and sizzled. She didn't seem to notice. She pulled out her half-full cup, replaced the coffeepot on top of the drops of liquid sizzling and burning on the warmer, and took a long swallow of the steaming coffee.

I winced and so did Erica. That had to hurt.

But Ms. Feld said, "Ah. That's better." She drained the cup on the second swallow (watching this made my own throat and stomach burn), rinsed the cup out, and set it in the drainboard. Then she gave us a sunny smile. "Okay, then. Let's get started."

Silently, we trailed after Ms. Feld to the children's room.

"Story time," she said briskly. "Monday through Fridays, eleven A.M. to noon at the latest. Tuesdays and Thursdays we read picture books. Mondays and Wednesdays we read short chapter books for a slightly older audience. Fridays are for children of all ages to listen to Storybook Wanda, a professional storyteller who volunteers her time."

Before we could ask questions, Ms. Feld pointed to one corner of the room where pillows and a few munchkin chairs were scattered over an area with its own dark blue plush carpeting. A platform with a big armchair facing outward occupied the extreme corner. Next to the armchair was a small table. To one side of the platform were two stacks of more chairs, one stack also munchkin-sized, the other adult-sized.

Although I don't get along with textbooks, I like the children's room at the library. When I was little, children had to go to the second floor to a shabbier, darker room that had a few child-sized chairs and a couple of those posters of the award-winning books that librarians like to recommend to children instead of Nancy Drew. This newer room is really two rooms that take up one window-paneled corner of the first floor of the library. The main room holds the children's librarian's desk, the card catalog computer, and the fiction section. In the smaller room, there are two newly acquired computers that kids can sign up to use, along with all of the nonfiction books. Both rooms are full of books, and nooks and crannies where kids can curl up and read. The smaller room even has a puppet theater. A giant Raggedy Ann doll, just waiting to be cuddled, sits on one of the child-sized chairs. Most of the read-this-award-winning-book posters have been replaced by cool prints of illustrations from picture books. I recognized several artists' work that I admired and saw a few that were new to me.

But before I could grab a chance to examine the new artists, Ms. Feld stepped in. "Why don't you two arrange the story corner to get started? Adult chairs in a semicircle in the back, smaller chairs in front of those, and pillows on the floor — facing the platform, of course. When you're finished there, I'll show you how to shelve books. We don't ask the children to return the books to the shelves. It leads to chaos, since some of them are too young to under-stand the shelving system. Enjoy!" She wiggled her fingers, beamed, and adjusted her flight pattern to-ward her glassed-in cubicle by the door.

Dazed and potentially confused, I glanced at Erica. She grinned. "Let's enjoy!" she said.

*   *   *

The place was a zoo. It was eleven-fifteen, and I couldn't decide whether these were children or human jumping beans. It's not that I didn't know how to handle a bunch of little kids. I did. I just didn't know which of them were my responsibility.

Although story time officially began at eleven, it quickly became clear that we weren't on a strict schedule. Ms. Feld stood to one side of the platform, holding several picture books and a large brass bell. She was talking to a thin man with a plump baby slung in a baby carrier in front of him. The baby was asleep, amazingly enough. I say *amazingly* because although this was a library, it was anything but quiet. I decided that the children's room must be sound-proofed at the very least. Otherwise, adult patrons would be slamming through the door, expecting to find a riot.

And they wouldn't be far from wrong.

Towers of books were stacked on all the tables. A few children flipped the pages. One little girl, holding a book about Big Bird upside down, was pretending to read and laughing hysterically. A boy wearing what looked like parts of several Halloween costumes had commandeered Raggedy Ann and was dragging her around by the arm.

I saw it coming but couldn't stop the inevitable.

As he crossed the room toward the puppet theater, Raggedy Ann's feet swept out and a much smaller boy tripped and went down on his bottom.

The little boy's brown cheeks turned ruddy, and he began to scream.

I reached him at the same time his mother did. "Ricardo," she said. "Why are you crying?"

"The doll kicked me!" he howled.

"A doll can't kick you," his mother said, picking him up matter-of-factly and setting him on his feet.

"Story hour is about to begin," I said brightly to Ricardo. "Why don't you pick out a chair just your size to sit in. Remember how Goldilocks had to try all three of the bears' chairs before she found one that was just the right size?"

"Bears," he said, sniffling his tears away.

He picked a chair in the front and center. Then he made his mother sit on it so he could sit on her lap. Her knees were folded up almost to her chin. Ricardo squeezed in somehow and settled back, looking pleased with himself. His mother's eyes met mine, and she smiled and winked.

Ms. Feld took her place in the reader's chair. She'd put on a pink sweater, which was buttoned wrong, making her seem more like one of the children than the librarian.

As soon as she sat down the children began to drift toward her from all over the room. Although I wouldn't have thought it possible, the noise level increased.

Ms. Feld put the bell on the table and arranged the books. Then she picked up the bell and rang it loudly.

Silence fell. Every face turned in her direction.

"Welcome to Stoneybrook Story Time," she said, smiling. "We're going to have a few wonderful stories today. One is a fairy tale . . . does everybody know what a fairy tale is?"

"Goldilocks!" said Ricardo.

"Beauty and the Beast," another child piped up.

That set off a storm of voices volunteering the titles of tales. Ms. Feld listened, then held her finger to her lips. Gradually, the room grew quiet again.

"Very good," she said. "I see you know all about fairy tales. This is a fairy tale that many of you probably have heard. It's about a giant . . . and some magic beans. Does anyone know what it is?"

She held up the picture book.

The cry of "JACK AND THE BEANSTALK" could probably have been heard all the way across town.

I glanced at the door, but no one came in to protest.

Ms. Feld began to read. This was a different Ms. Feld, one who read slowly and clearly, who changed her voice to sound like all the different characters and who patiently held up the pictures for the children to see. The children on the floor crept closer and closer as she read, and other children slid out of chairs and laps to be closer too. Soon most of the chairs were empty, and almost every child was as close to Ms. Feld as he or she could get without actually being in the librarian's lap.

I admit it. I was spellbound too.

Then Ms. Feld looked up, met my eyes, and nodded in the direction of the door to the children's room. I looked over at it again just as it began to close. I caught a glimpse of scarlet.

Omigosh. One of the children had not been as spellbound as I had been. Feeling that I'd fallen down on the job, I ran (discreetly) to the door and opened it. A girl of about five, in red overalls and a red-and-white-striped T-shirt, was trotting down the hall, a book under one arm.

"Hey," I said, and then recognized her. It was six-year-old Laurel Kuhn, one of our regular baby-sitting clients. "Hey, Laurel!"

She turned. "Hi, Claudia."

"Where are you going, Laurel?"

She shrugged. "Those are baby stories. Patsy likes them, but I'm too big for them." Laurel has always believed that she is much more mature than her five-year-old sister, Patsy.

I saw that the book tucked under her arm was *Black Beauty*. I was pretty sure she wasn't quite up to reading that yet. But I said, "You like *Black Beauty*?"

"Mom's reading it to us. I'm going to find her so she can read some more of it."

"Your mom's in the library?"

"In the music section. She told us to wait in the children's room. Jake's at the computer, playing some kind of computer soccer game. And Patsy's listening to Ms. Feld read baby stories." She shrugged.

I put my hand on her shoulder. "Let's go back into the children's room and wait for your mom there, with your sister and brother."

A mulish expression came over Laurel's face. I went on, "You can help me. Today is the first day of my job working at the library, and I need a grown-up kid to help me keep an eye on the other — the little kids — okay?"

Laurel eyed me. Then she said, "Okay."

We returned to the children's room. Ms. Feld had started to read one of my favorite books, *A Baby Sister for Frances*. It's about a badger child coping with the arrival of a new baby in the family, and it is very funny.

Erica approached me. "Good catch," she whispered.

"Ms. Feld saw her leave — even though she was reading. She's amazing."

"Radar. They install it in all librarians and teachers," Erica assured me. "I'll help you keep an eye on the door."

In spite of herself, Laurel had begun to listen to the adventures of Frances. It was clearly a favorite of several children, who said the lines right along with Ms. Feld.

The story hour went smoothly after that, if you don't count a chair-tipping-and-howls (no injuries except to pride) and the baby in the baby carrier waking up and bursting into tears.

Through it all, Ms. Feld stayed calm, cool, and collected.

When the story hour ended, the children more or less stormed the checkout desk. At the same time, a separate wave of children broke for the door. I made sure that all of the children were with their parents (extensive baby-sitting experience helped here, since I recognized many of them).

When I'd gotten them sorted out, I turned with a sigh of relief.

Ms. Feld, radar at full force, said, "Claudia? I sent Erica to check on the nonfiction room to make sure no children had wandered in there. When she gets back, why don't you two start reshelving the books?"

"Sure," I said.

Then I registered exactly how much work that meant. Books stood heaped on and under every table and almost every chair. They were scattered around the library like big squares of confetti from some giant's crazy party. The library couldn't have looked more upside down if a hurricane had blown through it.

Erica and I worked at top speed all day. Helping in the children's library is like baby-sitting with lots of extra books. No matter how many times we put books away, they somehow magically returned to the tables, chairs, and floor.

At four o'clock, Ms. Feld said, "Well, it's slowing down now. We close the children's room at five today, so why don't you go home."

I was more relieved than I liked to admit.

"Thanks," I said with a gasp, and staggered toward the door and freedom.

"I'm going to stick around awhile," Erica said as we made our escape.

I looked at her in surprise. "You're kidding, right?"

"No."

"Why? Aren't you wiped out?"

"I'm fine." She laughed. "Although if someone huffed and puffed they could pretty much blow me down right now. No, I want to stay and . . ." She looked around, then lowered her voice. "Do a little research."

"Research? It's summer. No homework, remember?"

"Not that." Erica shook her head and leaned closer. "I want to use the library computers to try to find my birth parents. I want to know their names, who they were."

I didn't know what to say. I knew Erica had been adopted.

"Do your parents know you're going to search?" I said.

"Well, they know I want to know who and where my birth parents are. But you've heard what they say — I'm not old enough, I need to wait, the time will come. But I don't want to wait. I'm ready to know *now*."

For half a second I was reminded of Laurel Kuhn's insistence on her grown-up status.

"Don't tell," Erica went on. "Not anyone."

"Of course not!" I said, stung that she'd think I would rat her out. "I'll even help, if I can."

"Thanks. I'll let you know if I need it."

Erica headed toward the computers.

I headed for the door. It had been a busy, exhausting day, and I didn't really want to think about Erica's secret search. But I couldn't help wondering if she was doing the right thing.

❀ Chapter 4

Day two at the library was a repeat of day one. I worked on processing a huge stack of books for Ms. Feld. Somewhere in the stacks, Erica was shelving the last of the books that had been left by the whirlwind of children who had spent a constructive and, er, creatively messy story hour in the children's room earlier.

The room had emptied out at lunchtime. After a short break, Erica and I went to work putting it back into some semblance of order.

I pasted a card pocket into the back of a new picture book, paused to admire the art, then set it to one side. After I'd finished putting a card pocket into the back of every new book, I'd stamp each one with the name of the library. By then, Erica would probably be through with shelving, and she could help me wrap the books in protective plastic covering.

After that, the books would be entered into the library's computer tracking system, and then they'd be shelved.

Paste. Smooth. Set aside. Paste. Smooth. Set aside.

"Hey there. What's a big girl like you doing in the children's room?"

I looked up. Alan Gray was standing there. "Alan! What are *you* doing here?"

He shrugged. "I kind of heard you might be around." He paused. "I called your house and a girl told me that there was a 'strong probability that you would be at the Stoneybrook Library's children's room, since that is where you are currently employed.'"

I had to laugh. "That's my sister, Janine. She talks like that sometimes. I used to think it was just because she was a genius and couldn't help it, but now I think she likes it because it throws other people off balance."

"A genius, huh?" Alan looked around. "You'd have to be pretty smart to work here too."

Now that made me feel good. It isn't often a girl like me, who is what teachers call an "underachiever," gets called smart, except in sentences that begin, "Claudia seems smart, but she just doesn't want to try." That's how my teachers see me. And how smart can you appear when you live in a family with a genuine genius? It isn't easy.

I gave Alan a big smile.

He smiled back, a polite, nongoofy smile. He didn't look like Alan when he did it. It was almost weird. He said, "So, can I help with anything?"

"Everything's under control," I replied. I glanced toward the cubicle where Ms. Feld was sorting a huge stack of papers into smaller stacks around her desk.

I'd finished the pasting. I'd give the books a few minutes to dry and then stamp them with the library stamp. I began to gather the materials together to return them to the supply cabinet.

"Here, let me help," said Alan.

"It's okay. I've got it."

"No, I don't mind. Really." He smiled that smile again. It just wasn't natural. It looked, well, fake. Non-Alan.

After the things had been put away, I looked for Erica. Alan went with me.

Erica gave him a curious look but only said, "Hi, Alan."

"Hello, Erica. How are you? Are you having a good day?"

"Uh, sure," Erica answered.

"I thought I'd help you shelve books. Then we can finish processing the new books," I said.

Erica nodded. I took some books from the cart and walked to the next aisle and began to slot them into their correct places on the shelves. Alan went right along with me. We were in the juvenile fiction section, where the shelves are normal height. The picture-book shelves are only two shelves high, just the right size for very young readers.

"*Fell*," Alan read aloud from a book he'd taken from the shelf. "By M. E. Kerr. It's a mystery. Is it any good?"

"Mmm," I said. "She's a great writer." I hadn't read any of her books, but I remembered my friend Mallory, who reads *everything*, raving about her. "My favorite mysteries are Nancy Drews."

There. I'd said it aloud. In a library.

Nothing terrible happened to me.

"Nancy Drew? You would like her, being an artist," Alan said. I looked puzzled. He said, "Nancy *Drew*, get it?"

"Oh." I smiled. That was a little more like the Alan I knew. "Not bad, Alan."

"Thank you." His smile was a little more Alan-like now. But it faded to a serious look as he said, "Here, let me help you put those away." He reached for the books. And somehow the whole stack slipped from my grasp and slid to the floor with a crash.

Erica's voice came from the next aisle. "You guys okay?"

"Fine," I said quickly. "Just dropped some books."

We both bent to retrieve the books. Our heads — believe it or not — actually cracked together.

I rocked back on my heels with a yelp. I think Alan did the same.

Rubbing my forehead and blushing, I said, "Alan. I'm almost through for today. You don't have to help me finish up."

The old Alan would probably have pretended he needed brain surgery or something, maybe rolled around on the floor. The new Alan took the hint. "I'll wait and walk you home, then," he said. "See you outside." He hesitated. "I'm really sorry, Claudia. I didn't mean to be so clumsy. Are you hurt?"

Alan was apologizing. Hmm.

"I'm fine. No big deal. See you in a little while," I said quickly.

"Great." He headed for the door. I thought I saw

him rubbing his forehead on the way through it.

I finished shelving books. Then it was quitting time.

"See you tomorrow, Ms. Feld," I said, stopping in the door of her office. She looked up and smiled.

"You girls are doing a wonderful job," she said.

"It's pretty wonderful being here," I replied truthfully. I paused and added, "Ms. Feld, I was noticing that the mural on the wall outside the children's room is looking a little faded and out-of-date."

"It is, isn't it?" She grimaced.

"Yes," I went on, "and I was wondering if you'd like someone to touch it up a little, maybe modernize it a bit."

"Did you have anyone in mind?"

"Me," I said.

"Claudia's an outstanding artist," Erica put in. "She's won awards. She's amazingly talented."

I blushed and gave Erica a grateful glance. "I could bring in some examples of my work," I said.

"That would be lovely," said Ms. Feld. "Redoing the mural is a fantastic idea, Claudia."

"I'll bring in some of my artwork tomorrow," I said. "If you like it, I can draw a new design, and we can talk about it." I was trying hard to sound professional and not show how excited I was. My fingers fairly itched to get to work on the mural.

"Lovely," Ms. Feld said, and went back to work on her papers. "Don't forget to put the 'Please ring bell for librarian' sign at the checkout desk."

"Got it," Erica said.

We headed out of the library. But before we reached the front door, Erica veered off. "I'm going to see if I can find any books by people who've looked for their birth parents," she said.

"I know one," I said. "But it's fiction."

"What is it?"

"*Find a Stranger, Say Good-bye*. It's by Lois Lowry."

Erica whipped a notebook out of her backpack and wrote it down. "Thanks," she said. "See you tomorrow."

"Good luck," I answered.

Then I went outside to walk home with Alan. I was glad to see him. But I didn't want to see anybody I knew. That would require some explanations I wasn't ready to make quite yet.

Oh, well. I could just say I'd run into him accidentally. That was more or less true. I had the bump on the head to prove it.

Chapter 5

My mother was silent all the way to the library the next morning. I didn't notice. I was immersed in mental art — trying out ideas in my head for the new mural for the library.

She pulled into the spot marked KISHI in the employee section of the parking lot and stopped. "Claudia," she said.

"Hmmm?" My hand was on the door.

"I wish you hadn't gone behind my back to talk to Ms. Feld about redoing the mural."

"What?" I was truly surprised.

"Dolores stopped by my office yesterday afternoon on her way home. She was very enthusiastic about your suggestion. And delighted that you'd volunteered to do it. I appreciate your initiative, Claudia, but that's not why you were hired. And you should have spoken to me first."

"Sorry," I said, sounding snappish. Why was my mother going off on this big power trip? Why did she have to be so negative about my art? I went on, "It won't happen again. I just let my enthusiasm for a terrific idea get the best of me."

There was a definite edge to my voice. My mother glanced at me. "It is a good idea," she said evenly. "But . . ."

"Don't worry. I won't embarrass you. I'm a good artist, even if I'm not some genius."

It was an unfair thing to say and I knew it. But I hated that she had ruined my excitement. I jumped out of the car before my mom could answer. "I have to get to work," I said, and raced up the library steps to join Ms. Feld, who was just unlocking the front door.

I avoided my mother for the rest of the day, which was easy to do since she stays pretty busy in the main part of the library. Avoiding Alan, even if I'd wanted to (and about that I had mixed feelings), wasn't as easy. He stopped by again that day, right after story hour. And he had a fantastic time in the puppet theater with some of the kids. Unfortunately, when he got the idea of sticking crayons in his mouth to make monster teeth, all the little kids wanted to do it too. We had to remove quite a few crayons from quite a few mouths (and settle a few rebellious tantrums).

"Sorry," Alan said as I persuaded the last little girl that she would much rather take the Raggedy Ann doll on a walk to look for a picture book than play with crayons for the moment.

"No problem," I said. "Piece of cake for an experienced baby-sitter like me."

I grinned at him and he grinned back, more of the old Alan grin this time than the formal smile he'd been using lately.

"I guess I better go," he said. "Before I cause any more trouble."

"Don't worry about it. You were great with the kids."

"Probably because I think like one."

What could I say to that? I settled on, "Well, thanks for stopping by."

"Anytime."

At my lunch break, I stayed in the children's room rather than going to the staff break room. Not only did I not want to see my mother just yet, but I had work to do. I got out my sketch pad and worked on the mural design. The next afternoon, when my mom would be in the Friday staff meeting, I'd go outside and draw a copy of the mural to work with. I'd already put a folder with samples of my art in Ms. Feld's in-box, but I knew she'd been too busy to look at it yet. When she did, I wanted to be ready with some of my ideas for the mural.

And I wanted those ideas to be brilliant. I'd show my mother.

Erica had slipped into the nonfiction room. I could see part of her back through the door. She was tapping away at the computer, scrolling down what looked like a list. I knew she was deep into research on her birth parents. Something about the way she was hammering at the keys told me she wasn't having much success yet.

I stared down at the blank paper in front of me. *Books,* I thought. *Libraries. Reading.*

As I have mentioned, these are not subjects that appeal to me all that much outside of Nancy Drew. I remembered posters I'd seen, designed to encourage kids to read — awesome art by artists like Maurice Sendak.

Relax, I told myself. You don't have to be Sendak. You just have to be Kishi.

But by Friday, I still hadn't come up with an idea I liked. Nor did Erica seem any happier with her research. And my mother and I were keeping a pretty chilly distance between us. I was glad my first week of work was almost over. I was going to need the entire weekend to recover.

Then Alan dropped by just before quitting time.

I was gathering up puzzle pieces from on, beneath, and all around the table in the puzzle corner. This wasn't easy, because two jigsaw puzzles had been mixed together. Fortunately, one was a brightly colored dinosaur picture and the other used a more pastel palette that involved Cinderella.

I saw Alan's feet first. "Hey," he said.

I backed out from beneath the table. "Hi, Alan. Hold on a sec." I ducked back under the table and retrieved the last few pieces. I backed out again.

This time, Alan *and* Kristy were standing there. Uh-oh.

"You could go outside and watch the grass grow," Kristy suggested to Alan.

"Oh, really?" Alan's eyebrows went up. "Is that how you spend your time?"

"Hi, guys," I said. "Can I recommend any books for you? You'll have to make your selection quickly, though. The library closes in fifteen minutes."

Kristy, who looked more than a little steamed that Alan had zinged her, said, "The picture books are over there, Alan."

Alan said to me, "I read *Fell*."

"*Fell*," I repeated blankly.

"The book you recommended. By M. E. Kerr."

"I did?" I said.

"You said she was an excellent writer. She is. And there are more books about the same character. His name is Fell and he . . ."

"Claudia's a little busy right now for a book report, Alan," said Kristy.

I'd been looking at Alan, feeling deeply flattered that he'd read the book, even though I hadn't exactly recommended it. (Mallory had, really.) Kristy's words jerked me back to the unpleasant situation developing between Alan and Kristy — with me in the middle.

He smiled. Hugely. "When you learn to read, Kristy," he said, "I recommend it."

Kristy began to sputter. I said quickly, "You guys, stop it. If you're going to fight, go outside."

"We're not fighting," said Kristy. "I do *not* engage in battles of wit with the unarmed."

"Stop it," I said, my voice sounding very stern and librarian-ish. "This is a library and this is my job. So behave. Both of you."

"Sorry," said Alan.

"Sorry," Kristy mumbled.

"If you'll excuse me," I said, "I have work to do." I walked away. It was a coward's thing to do, but so what? Sometimes it's better to walk away.

Kristy said in a loud voice, "I'll wait outside, Claudia. We can walk to the BSC meeting together."

"Right," I said, pretending that going through the reserved-book cards was the most important thing I had to do in the world. When I looked up again, Kristy and Alan were both gone. And to my relief, only Kristy was waiting for me on the steps outside.

"Sorry," she said again. "But Alan is a world-class jerk."

"He's not so bad," I said. "You two just rub each other the wrong way."

"That's the understatement of the year!" Kristy snorted.

What could I say?

I said, "We'd better hurry. We're going to be late."

That got Kristy's attention.

She didn't mention Alan again all the way to my house. She was too busy looking at her watch, reporting the time and telling me to walk faster.

❀ Chapter 6

But I might have known she wouldn't let the matter drop.

She called the meeting to order and said, "You know, Claudia, it could ruin your reputation."

"What could ruin Claud's reputation?" asked Dawn, intrigued.

"Being seen with the wrong people. Wait, being seen with the wrong *species*," Kristy said.

"What are you talking about, Kristy?" asked Mary Anne.

"Kristy ran into Alan at the library today, and they exchanged the usual compliments," I intervened. "You know, she told him he should be looking for something to read in the picture book section and he implied that she didn't know how to read at all. Very mature."

Stacey's eyebrows went up. Dawn let out a soundless whistle. Mary Anne said, "Oh, Kristy."

"He is *such* a jerk."

"He hasn't worn underwear on his head in school since second grade," I said, torn between laughter and despair.

That surprised a snicker of laughter from Kristy (and Dawn and Stacey). Mary Anne continued to look distressed.

"You know," Kristy said, "it's one thing to go to a dance with him because of a mix-up. I'll even admit he more or less behaved himself. But if you keep being seen with him, people are going to think you're really interested in him, and you don't want that to happen."

Stacey looked at me, then at Kristy, then down at her feet.

The phone rang. Everyone seemed to let out a little sigh of relief as Kristy fielded the call. But as soon as she hung up, Kristy returned, like a terrier to a bone, to the same subject. "And don't try to defend him, Claudia. It'll make me suspicious that you're actually thinking of going out with Alan."

I couldn't take it any longer. "I am," I said. "I mean, I *have*."

"Good for you," Stacey said softly.

Kristy's face turned bright red. "WHAT?"

Dawn said neutrally, "You're shouting, Kristy."

"I AM NOT."

We all looked at her. Although it didn't seem possible, her face grew redder. She took a deep breath. Was it possible? Was Kristy Thomas about to explode, actually explode, in Technicolor, here in my bedroom?

She let out her breath. Her face turned a less alarming shade of red. "Claudia," she said in the voice of a baby-sitter reasoning with the ax murderer she's just discovered in the linen closet, "Alan Gray is not possible. You must see that."

"I see him as . . . possible," I said brightly. Inside I was raging. But, in a perverse way, I was also enjoying goading Kristy.

"Claudia," said Kristy, her voice even more level. (At any moment I expected her to say, "Drop the ax. We can work this out.") "I would be totally supportive of your going out with anybody, *anybody* . . . except Alan Gray. When Stacey went out with Sam — did I say a word?"

"Well, actually — " Stacey began, and I knew she was recalling Kristy's reaction when one of her friends went out with her big brother.

Kristy held up her hand majestically. "When you

and Stacey were fighting over a boy, did I say a word?"

"In that particular case, you — " Stacey tried again.

"But now . . . *now*, I can't in good conscience keep quiet. Claudia, think about what you're doing. You're going to get hurt. Ridiculed. Frustrated. You think he's changed, but boys like Alan don't change."

"He hasn't changed," I said. "He's just more himself with me."

"It happens, Kristy," Mary Anne said. "Why don't you give Alan a chance?"

"Or at least give Claudia a chance to give Alan a chance?" Dawn put in.

"Right," Stacey said. "Kristy, you — "

"Listen to me, people. This is serious. Alan Gray is not date material. He's not even human material."

Stacey finally got a full sentence in, and it was a punch. "Kristy," she said, "according to my information, you yourself went out with Alan Gray once."

That stopped Madame President.

"To a dance," I added.

"It's true," Mary Anne said as Dawn gave a yelp of laughter.

Kristy's face went beet-red again. But she didn't admit defeat, she just said, "The point is, I learned my lesson. I never went to a dance with him again. Benefit from my experience, Claudia. Don't do this to yourself."

The phone rang again. I wanted to laugh. I wanted to cry. I wanted to scream.

I wanted to leave.

"Baby-sitters Club," Kristy said, her voice still unnaturally soothing and calm.

Her next reaction was pure baby-sitter-meets-ax-murderer-and-loses-it. "What?" she screeched. "Absolutely do not call here during club business hours again, or you'll be deeply and permanently sorry!"

She slammed the phone down so hard that it jumped.

So did the rest of us.

"Kristy?" I said. "That phone is mine. You break it, you buy it."

She turned her wrathful face toward me. "It was Alan," she said through gritted teeth.

As an artist, I could appreciate the color her face had turned. I didn't know it was humanly possible.

As a person, I resented her attitude. She was being bossy, unreasonable, and typically Kristy. But this time, I wasn't going to let her push me around.

"Alan can call here," I said frostily. "It's *my*

phone in *my* room in *my* house. You don't have the right to hang up on him."

"He called during *our* meeting," Kristy answered, just as frostily.

"I'll request that he refrain from calling during our meetings in the future."

"Do that," said Kristy. "Refrain him."

We glared at each other.

Mary Anne glanced at the clock on my desk. "Oops. Six o'clock!"

"This meeting of the Baby-sitters Club is now *adjourned*!" Kristy barked. She stood up and stalked out of my room.

"It'll work out," Mary Anne said.

"Ha," I said.

We heard a door slam.

"The coast is clear," Dawn said cheerfully. "Well, this *has* been an interesting meeting."

Somehow, I sensed that Dawn wasn't taking this too seriously.

"Glad you enjoyed it," I said as she and Mary Anne departed.

Stacey left last. She said, "Claudia, I'm glad you told Kristy."

"Yeah. But I don't think it helped anything. In

fact, I might have made matters worse. What's Kristy going to do to Alan when she sees him now?"

Stacey laughed. "I think Alan can take care of himself. In fact, no matter what you think of Alan, you've got to admit that he has one thing in his favor."

"What's that?" I said.

"He's one of the few people around who isn't afraid of Kristy." Stacey gave me a sweet smile and walked out, closing the door softly behind her.

❋ Chapter 7

The phone rang.

I knew it was Alan. I picked it up. "Hello?"

Talking through his nose, Alan said, "Baby-sitters Club, have I got a baby for you! How long do you sit on them before they hatch?"

"Alan," I said.

"How'd you guess?" He laughed heartily.

Maybe at another time I would have thought he was funny. Okay, mildly amusing. But at the moment I was just annoyed. For this I was having a fight with my friend?

"Alan," I said, "now's not a good time."

"How about Sunday night, then?"

"What?"

"How about a good time on Sunday — like a movie-dinner good time?"

I hesitated, torn between annoyance with him and anger at Kristy.

"If you'll agree, I'll hang up the phone quietly," Alan said.

"Okay," I told him, maybe just a tad ungraciously.

"See you Sunday," he said, and hung up.

I hung up too, more confused than ever. I'd had a fight with Kristy, shocked the entire BSC, and wasn't even sure I wanted to go out with Alan.

I could hardly wait for Sunday.

Or maybe I could hardly wait for Sunday to be over.

"Claudia." I opened our front door on Sunday evening, and Alan handed me a flower. But it wasn't just an ordinary flower. It was a carnation in an amazing number of colors, many of them completely unnatural.

"I thought, with your artist's eye, you'd appreciate my attempt to improve on nature," Alan said, almost as if he'd read my thoughts.

"It's — amazing," I said. I smelled the carnation. The sweet spicy scent was still there. It was still a carnation in spite of its outward appearance. "How did you do this?"

"Split the stem about six different ways and stuck little test tubes of colored water on the end of each one. It wasn't easy. But you're worth it." Alan was laughing, but something about the way he said it made me blush.

I turned hastily away. "Let me just put this in some plain water, and I'll be right back."

When I returned to the front door, he was talking to my mother. I heard her say, "Won't you come in, Alan?"

She gave me a disapproving look and I could see she thought I'd been rude not to invite Alan in.

And she was right. But honestly, at that moment I was so confused about so many things that I'd forgotten. I really had.

Alan didn't seem to mind. "Thank you, but our ride is waiting." He motioned behind him, and I saw a man in a car at the curb. "My dad," Alan said. "He's going to drop us off at the movie and pick us up afterward."

"Have fun." My mother gave Alan a smile. I wasn't sure if I was included. Things were still pretty tense between us.

"We will," Alan assured her.

We didn't talk much until we were in our seats at the theater. Alan glanced around. "Sundays aren't big movie nights, are they? I guess you always get a good seat."

I said abruptly, "Alan. About calling during the club meetings. Could you not do that? It . . . it upsets Kristy."

"Really?" he said innocently. He leaned back and turned to look at me. "Gee, I'm sorry."

Part of me wanted to laugh. Another part of me was annoyed. "Your crank calls mean that fewer of our clients can get through to us," I continued.

"You're calling me a business liability?"

I wasn't sure what that meant. "No," I said. "But if you keep it up, I'll be calling you a real pain." I smiled when I said it, so it wouldn't hurt Alan's feelings.

He raised his eyebrows. The house lights went down.

"Only fifteen minutes of commercials until movie time," I said.

"Yeah," said Alan.

"Good grief! Look at that. Those are the same lame commercials as the last time we were here. They could at least change them."

"Never overestimate the intelligence of the public. That's what P. T. Barnum said, more or less."

I thought about that for a minute. "You mean

someone is saying that most people are so stupid it doesn't matter how many times you show them the same commercial?"

"That's it," Alan said. He looked thoughtful. Then he went on. "Barnum owned a circus. I just read a book about him. I think it would be cool to have a circus."

"I can see it," I said.

Alan turned toward me. "Not just so I could be a clown."

"I didn't mean that," I said. But the truth was, I had envisioned exactly that: Alan in a clown suit, with a big nose and bulbous shoes and one of those gag flowers that squirts water in your face when you sniff it.

"Not that there's anything wrong with clowns," Alan went on.

"Of course not."

Behind us, someone said, "Shhh!"

So we weren't the only ones in the theater. We didn't talk after that. But I kept thinking about Alan, kept seeing him as a clown in the middle of a three-ring circus. Was that what Alan really was at heart? Was the old Alan lurking somewhere inside, his clown suit hidden beneath a cloak of good behavior?

When the movie ended, we walked to Pizza

Express. It was still light outside, and at Alan's suggestion we took the pizza to the covered patio strung with fake grapevines and crammed with wooden plank tables topped by red-and-white-checked plastic tablecloths.

I scanned the patio as we sat down.

"Looking for someone?" Alan asked.

"No," I said quickly. "Just looking. It's a nice night."

I sounded like my mother, talking about the weather. I sat down and grabbed a slice of pizza.

"Careful, it's — "

I crammed the pizza in my mouth and let out a glooey yelp. As I gulped soda, Alan finished, " — hot. Are you okay, Claudia?"

I nodded. When I could talk again, I said, "I should have known it would be too hot."

We ate in silence for a moment. Several times, Alan looked as if he were about to speak, but he didn't.

"Good pizza," I said finally, just to say something.

"My favorite," Alan said. "I love anchovies."

I let out another yelp. "Anchovies. I *hate* anchovies." I jerked the slice of pizza away from my mouth and let it drop onto the plate. Bending over, I examined it. "Great. I must have eaten all the anchovies on this slice. Ugh. I can't believe I didn't taste them. I — "

I looked up. Alan was laughing.

"Claudia," he said, "there are no anchovies."

"No . . . oh." I didn't know whether to laugh or smack Alan with the pizza slice. Starting a food fight, however, was beneath my dignity. (Although, as Kristy might have observed, it probably wasn't beneath Alan's.)

"I was just teasing, Claudia," Alan said.

"Right." I smiled. If anybody else had pulled that on me, I probably would have laughed.

But if I laughed at Alan, I might just encourage him. And who knew where that might lead — to an impromptu dance with the pizza pan on his head? A burping demonstration? A display of his ability to squirt soda out of his nose?

"I guess I fell for it. Good one." To my own ears, I sounded like a baby-sitter talking to a bratty little kid. I hoped I didn't sound like that to Alan. He gave me a long look, but he didn't say anything.

When Alan's father arrived to pick us up, I admit I was relieved. I forced another smile for Alan's slam-dunk of the paper plates and napkins into the trash can while I slid the pizza pan onto the busboy's tray. But I couldn't think of anything to say.

We rode to my house in silence.

"Thanks," I said when I got out. "It was fun."

"It was?" Alan said. I had the sudden, uncomfortable feeling that he knew exactly what I was thinking.

But that wasn't possible. Was it?

"See you later," I went on.

"I hope so," said Alan. But his voice was cool, careful. Very un-Alan.

I hurried into the house. The car pulled away.

Upstairs in my room, I flopped on my bed. I'd been on worse dates, but few that had felt so awkward. How had that happened? Up until tonight, I'd enjoyed Alan's company and I was pretty sure he had enjoyed mine.

But tonight, he'd been stiff, awkward. And that had made me feel the same way.

Or did I make Alan feel weird? Had he picked up on my nervousness about being seen with him?

That would be a first, I told myself. Someone else making weird Alan feel weird.

I knew I wasn't being fair. But I was tired. And confused. How could I go out with somebody if I always had to worry about what he might do, or what other people might think?

It wasn't worth it.

It just wasn't worth it.

I told myself that over and over until I finally fell asleep.

❀ Chapter 8

"First let me tell you that everybody does *not* love a clown," I said as I walked into the break room in the basement of the library on Monday morning at precisely fifteen minutes before the doors opened.

Erica, who was sprawled on the couch, holding a cup of hot tea, looked up with a startled expression. "What?"

She looked exhausted. "You look tired," I said. "Are you okay?"

"Oh, I'm full of frustration, aggravation, and temptation," she answered, waving one hand. "But you go first. What's this about clowns in love?"

I made myself a cup of tea and sat down next to Erica. We had the lounge to ourselves. The faint smell of burned coffee told me that Ms. Feld had already come and gone.

"Not clowns in love," I corrected her. "At least I hope not. But this whole thing is turning into a circus."

"You're not making any sense," Erica said.

"Sorry. It's just that . . . well, I had a date with Alan this weekend. Last night. We went to the movies. And for pizza. And this is not the first time I've gone out with him. We went out last Monday too." I sounded as if I were making a confession.

Erica looked surprised but not disgusted. Which was a relief. "Wow," she said. "Who'd have guessed?"

I sighed. "I know. I know. Who could possibly go out with someone like Alan?"

"Well, his sense of humor is pretty . . . second grade . . . sometimes," Erica said. "But I don't think he's hopeless or anything."

"You don't?"

She took a sip of tea, thought for a moment, then shook her head. "Nope."

"Kristy does. She was totally freaked out when I told her. She did everything but call me a loser." Perhaps I exaggerated a little, but not much. "And I don't think she's going to be the only one who reacts that way. Alan Gray has been Alan the class joke since first grade."

"People change," Erica assured me. "And you shouldn't worry so much about what other people think. If they're going to pass judgment on you for something as harmless as going out with a guy who isn't Mr. Maturity, then they're not worth listening to."

"You think?" I said, feeling slightly better.

"I think," Erica agreed. Then she sighed.

"Your turn," I said. "What's up?"

"Nothing," she answered glumly. "I spent most of the week on the Web and on the phone. I learned a *lot* about the process of finding your birth parents. I read tons of stories about other peoples' reunions." She sighed again.

"But?"

"But legally there's nothing that I can do. I mean, a thirteen-year-old has no legal way to get the adoption agency to release adoption records. I have to have my parents' permission — and they're being totally stubborn and unreasonable about this."

"Yeah, I know," I said sympathetically. Had my mother apologized to me for the mural misunderstanding? I think not. She was being pretty stubborn and unreasonable herself. I mean, sure she was talking to me pleasantly enough now, but did she mean it? No. She was still annoyed, I could tell. And I was annoyed that she was annoyed. "Listen, if there is anything, I mean *anything* I can do to help . . ."

"Maybe you can. I might have another plan," Erica said.

"What?"

"I'll tell you if I have to put it into effect." Erica managed to look determined and mysterious at the same time.

"Okay." I sipped my tea, added another tea-spoon of sugar, and took another swig. Better.

Erica looked at her watch. "We should get going," she said. She finished her tea, rinsed out her mug, and set it on the drainboard.

"Two seconds," I said. I drank as much of my tea as I could (how *did* Ms. Feld swallow all that scald-ing coffee first thing in the morning?), poured the rest out, rinsed my own mug, and headed upstairs with Erica.

As we entered the children's room, Ms. Feld looked up from a box of books she was unpacking. "I just *love* opening big boxes of new books, don't you?" she said.

"Definitely," Erica agreed. "Like when you order books through the book clubs at school. I can't ever remember what I ordered, so it's sort of like getting a present."

I didn't say anything. Unwrapping boxes of books did not make it onto my list of "Things to Love."

Ms. Feld lifted out the last stack of books. Boxes covered the floor around her. Erica said, "I'll take these boxes down to recycling."

"Thanks, Erica," said Ms. Feld. "And you can see what we'll be doing this morning until the children arrive for story hour. Processing books!" She said this with so much enthusiasm that I almost felt excited about the idea myself. Almost.

Then Ms. Feld said something that did pump up my excitement. She looked at me and said, "And, Claudia, *guess what*! I've gotten the go-ahead for the mural. I'd like to get started on Wednesday, if that's okay with you."

How had she done that? Had my mom approved? Or had they taken a vote on Friday at the meeting? Had my mom been against it and been outvoted?

I didn't want to think about all the possibilities. I simply said, "Great! I've drawn up a couple of ideas that I think we can use. I'll show them to you."

"As soon as story time is over," Ms. Feld agreed.

Needless to say, the next couple of hours stretched on as if they were years. Whatever my mom might have had to say about the mural, it was going to happen now. My artwork was going to be permanently (or at least, pretty permanently) installed on the wall of the Stoneybrook Library. I admit, I was psyched.

I was even more pysched by Ms. Feld's reaction to the ideas and sketches I showed her. The old mural was a series of panels showing children reading in different places and situations: a child in a tree house, a child sprawled on a rug in front of a fireplace, a child in bed beneath the covers with a flashlight, a child in a rocking chair with her grandmother reading to her, a child in a porch swing. It was nice and pretty and sweet, except that all of the children looked much the same: pink-cheeked kids, the girls in frilly dresses, the boys in pants. I'd used the same motif, but the kids looked like the kids I know: dark-skinned, light-skinned, curly hair, straight hair, a girl (who looked a little like Kristy in overalls), a solemn boy sitting by his grandmother, an older kid reading to a younger kid in the porch swing. There was even a row of little kids in sunglasses on towels, reading at the beach.

Then I'd added different characters altogether — *real* characters. In the row of kids at the beach, for example, a seagull read *Jonathan Livingston Seagull*, a pelican read *The Enormous Fish*, and a crab read *Sandcastles*. Behind them, a girl in a red cloak with a hood, carrying a basket, walked by. From the basket several books stuck out: *Maps to Grandma's House*, *How to Survive in the Woods*, and *Never Trust a Wolf*. Up in the tree house, a nest full of baby robins each had a teeny-tiny book, except for one, whose mouth was open in complaint. Above the baby robin, a parent robin was swooping down with a book in its beak. In the background, far, far away, a princess in a tower with long golden hair read a book. In tiny letters on the cover of the book, I'd written, *The Princess's Guide to Building Ladders*. Beneath the porch swing, a large dog with glasses read *How to House-train Your Human*. In a corner, a frog with a crown on its head read *The True Story of the Frog Who Kissed a Princess*.

You get the idea.

Ms. Feld kept exclaiming, "Claudia, this is wonderful. So imaginative. So . . . wonderful! In fact, it's brilliant."

I blushed and grinned like an idiot. My mother might not appreciate my efforts to improve the library, but Ms. Feld sure did.

"We'll get the supplies — give me a list of exactly what you want — and on, let's say, Wednesday, we'll get started. Is Wednesday good for you?"

"Wednesday's great," I said. I wasn't sure my mom would be thrilled by this, but it was out of her hands now.

I spent the afternoon on a cloud. Ms. Feld had said I was brilliant. And brilliant was the same as being a genius, practically. Wasn't it?

But the euphoria didn't last. My white puffy cloud turned into a storm cloud just as my shift ended. I'd walked out of the children's room, casting a possessive look at "my" wall where "my" mural would soon be on display for everyone to see — and Alan came around the corner.

"Hi, Claudia," he said. "I've been waiting for you."

"Hi," I said. "Uh — is anything wrong?"

"Maybe," Alan said. "I have to talk to you."

❀ Chapter 9

Alan and I walked out of the library. I didn't speak and neither did he. It was *not* a comfortable silence.

I took a deep breath.

Alan gave a little cough.

I said, like a dope, "Nice day."

Alan said, "Yeah. I guess."

I announced, "I have to go to my BSC meeting, Alan."

"I'll walk with you," he said.

"No, that's okay. You don't have to do that."

Alan stopped and turned to face me. "Why not?"

"Why not? What do you mean, why not?" I said, stalling for time.

"Why don't you want me walking you to your

house, Claudia? Are you ashamed of me or something?"

"No!" I protested. "No, that's not it."

Alan looked at me steadily.

"No," I repeated. Only it sounded more like a question than a declaration.

"I think you are," Alan said. "I think you don't want your friends to see me with you."

I just stared at him. What could I say? I didn't have to answer anyway. The blush that was turning my face red was answer enough.

Without thinking, I began to walk fast, but I couldn't outrun my feelings. And Alan had it figured out. I was ashamed to be seen with him.

"So what I think you have to do," Alan said, "is give me a chance."

"What?" I'd been thinking so hard I'd almost forgotten he was there. I slowed my steps and glanced at him.

"Give me a chance. I want to figure out where we go from here. Maybe it's just friendship. Maybe it's something more. But you have to give me a chance. You have to be honest with your friends."

Alan was right. I knew it as soon as he said it. We'd reached my corner, and I slowed even more.

"Be honest. Don't forget, honesty is the best policy. Besides, like Mark Twain said, 'The fewer lies you tell, the less you have to remember,' " Alan concluded.

"I never thought about telling the truth in quite that way." I paused, then said, "You're right. But it's not that I'm ashamed of you, Alan. It's that, well, some of my friends are a little negative about you."

"They don't know me. So what about this? Why don't you and I go out with some of your friends? That way we can all put the past in the past and maybe you won't feel weird being seen with me."

Slowly I nodded. "I like it," I said. "And I know exactly who I'll start with."

Kristy answered her phone on the first ring. "It's me," I said.

"You're canceling the meeting?" she asked. Kristy doesn't waste words on courtesy when life-and-death issues are at stake.

"No," I reassured her. "I just wondered if you could come a little early. I need to talk to you."

"Okay," she said, and hung up.

She didn't even ask what I wanted to talk about. How could she *not* ask?

I will never truly understand how Kristy's mind works. And maybe that's a good thing.

Less than half an hour later, she was knocking on my bedroom door. I told her to come in and offered her a piece of the Rainforest Crunch chocolate bar I'd just unwrapped to help my thought processes.

She broke off a piece. "What's up?" she asked.

"This is the deal," I said. "I should be able to see whoever I want to see and unless they're bad for me, my friends — like you — should back me up."

Narrowing her eyes, Kristy said, "Is this about Alan Gray?"

"Yup."

Kristy folded her arms. "I just don't see you and Alan together."

"Whether it's a good match is for Alan and me to find out — without interference." I refused to back down.

I met Kristy's eyes. I didn't blink. She scowled. And then she backed down!

"All right, all right. I know I shouldn't pass judgment on you and Alan. In the abstract, it's totally your business who you date. Totally. It's just that Alan Gray . . . I mean, Claudia, that's going to be hard."

"Just work on keeping an open mind. That's all I'm asking."

"I'll try," said Kristy. "I promise."

I don't completely understand Kristy, but I do know this: When she promises something, she keeps her word. So that was the end of the discussion.

I offered her some more chocolate. Between us, we finished the bar before the meeting even began.

But we didn't starve. After Mary Anne, Dawn, and Stacey arrived, I hauled out little boxes of cereal and a half-finished bag of Oreos to keep up our strength while we fielded phone calls and scheduled baby-sitting jobs.

In between calls, I brought up Alan's idea that we all go out together.

Stacey said, "Great, Claudia. When?"

"I'd like that. I really would," Mary Anne chimed in.

Dawn was less enthusiastic. "I'm not a big Alan Gray fan," she said, clearly stalling for time.

"You don't have to be. I just want you to see — no, Alan and I just want you to see that there is a different side to him. You don't have to think he's perfect or anything."

"Oh, fine. I'll do it. It'll be interesting. I hope." Dawn smiled and we all looked at Kristy.

Kristy made a face. She writhed in her chair. She scratched her shoulder and bit her lip.

"Kristy?" I said.

"Okay," she mumbled.

"Great. I knew I could count on you all. Wednesday afternoon. Miniature golf. How does that sound?"

"I can hardly wait," Kristy said glumly.

I ignored her. Sometimes with Kristy, that's all you can do.

❀ Chapter 10

Wonderful Wednesday arrived at last. Why was Wednesday a wonderful day? Because of my group date with Alan?

Not exactly. No, it was wonderful because we were going to start the mural in the library.

My mother hadn't mentioned the mural and neither had I. We were speaking to each other a little more naturally, but we weren't all warm and fuzzy.

I had taken a batch of art supplies in on Tuesday and had given Ms. Feld a list of the materials I thought we would need. I reached the children's room the next morning to find Erica and Ms. Feld unpacking several enormous shopping bags. Not only had Ms. Feld bought everything on my list, but she'd gone wild in the brush department. There were at least a dozen little paintbrushes and a sackful of cans that had been washed out.

Seeing my puzzled look, Ms. Feld said, "The cans are for extra paint for the children. I think it would be a lovely idea if they participated in the mural project. In fact, that's what we're going to do this morning instead of story hour."

My heart sank. "Uh, Ms. Feld?" I said.

Erica gave me a sympathetic look. I could tell she understood my dilemma. On the one hand, it was a mural for the children. On the other hand, lots of little kids with lots of paintbrushes, even painting down low on the wall, was a recipe for disaster.

"They'll love it," Ms. Feld said enthusiastically. "Oh, Claudia, this is going to be outstanding! *Out-*standing!"

I decided not to argue. Even though I was the artist, she was the boss. So instead of voicing my doubts, I said, "We'll need lots of newspaper."

"I brought plenty," Ms. Feld replied.

"I brought newspaper too," Erica said. "And an old shirt."

"Good idea," I said. I'd taken the same precaution, bringing not only an old, paint-splattered T-shirt, but also old jeans and sneakers.

Ms. Feld stopped. "Oh," she said. "You're right. We don't want the children to get paint on their clothes." For a moment, her face fell. Then it brightened. "Wait here!" she said, and charged out of the children's room.

We watched her go. I shook my head. "I have a bad feeling about this," I said.

"It'll be all right," Erica replied. I gave her a Look and she grinned. "Besides, a little paint never hurt anybody."

I agreed. But I wasn't sure how many parents would feel the same. I said, "Let's start papering the hall with the newspaper. The more surface we cover, the less paint we'll have to clean up afterward."

Ms. Feld returned. She was holding an armful of napkins — enormous red paper napkins. "These were left over from the Christmas party last year," she announced. "We'll tuck them in everybody's collars to protect their shirts."

Maybe it would work, maybe it wouldn't. I decided to not worry about it and to concentrate on roughing out the mural on the wall. To begin, I drew a long bright blue line across the bottom, about two feet from the floor.

"What's that for?" asked Erica.

"It's the kids' paint zone," I explained. "They can paint whatever they want below the blue line. Above it, I'll be updating the mural."

If only it had been that simple.

We spent the first half of story time draping kids with napkin bibs. Claire Pike, who is five, demanded that she draw in purple, like in *Harold and the Purple Crayon*.

When I told her I didn't have purple paint, her face turned that alarming shade of red familiar to anyone who has ever baby-sat for Claire. But she didn't launch into the tantrum for which I had braced myself.

Instead she said in a stubborn voice, "Purple."

Rather than argue, I mixed a small amount of red and blue in one of the cans and gave it to her. This pleased her enormously. It also led to several other children demanding custom paint colors. I made a batch of pink, lime-green, and an alarming shade of orange before Ms. Feld called a halt and herded us out into the hall.

Did I say we plastered the hall with newspapers? It wasn't enough. In no time flat, Claire had turned over her purple paint and launched into a full-out tantrum. By the time I'd finished dealing with her, Jackie Rodowsky (known affectionately among members of the BSC as the Walking Disaster) had managed to trip over not one but two cans of paint, stumbling against the mural and leaving one long smear of blue and another of green.

"I'm sorry, Claudia," he said, his face dotted with freckles of paint.

"Don't worry," I said, wiping him down as best I could.

"But I ruined your picture," he said unhappily.

I looked at the mural. The smears of paint were front and center. "It's okay," I said. "I can fix it. Now, why don't you pick a spot below the blue line on the wall and paint anything you want."

Looking more cheerful, Jackie went back to work. He stepped in a puddle of paint and made a trail of inky blue footprints across the newspaper, but I let him go. I had other things to worry about.

"Hey! Hey, below the blue line. You're supposed to paint below the blue line," I heard Erica say.

When I turned, I saw Erica and a little girl I didn't recognize. The little girl had painted an enormous flowerlike object in red and pink so that it looked as if it were growing — no, exploding — up out of the blue line.

Somehow, I never got to start work on the mural. Erica and I spent the hour doing damage control.

And a quick glance in Ms. Feld's direction showed me that Ms. Feld was being pushed to the limit too. She was smiling and cheerful, but she had paint in her hair, on her knees, along the hem of her skirt, and down one side of her leg. One item that was paint-free was the napkin she'd tucked into the collar of her blouse for protection.

Painting brought out more than the artist in the children: They shouted and laughed and sang and shrieked and flung paint in all directions. They dipped their hands into the paint and smeared it on the wall, on themselves, and on one another.

It was hopeless. I looked at my watch, then held it up and pointed at it so that Ms. Feld could see. She understood instantly.

She clapped her hands together. "Boys, girls, it's time to . . ."

She didn't finish.

My mother came around the corner with Miss Ellway. "You'll have to keep the noise down, Dolores," my mother said. "We can hear you all the way over in the — " My mother stopped her sentence cold. She just stared.

"We were just about to start cleaning up for the day," said Ms. Feld brightly.

My mother's face was anything but bright. In

fact, it looked a little like a thundercloud. Her voice was way too calm and controlled as she said, "We'll help."

She clapped her hands and said in a quiet sort of roar, "Everybody listen to me!"

That got the attention of all the little Michelangelos and Georgia O'Keeffes. The noise subsided. Paint-daubed faces turned in my mother's direction.

"I want every one of you to put down your paintbrushes and your paint and step away from the mural."

At any other time, I would have found my mother's unconscious parody of a television police officer funny.

But not now.

In fact, I put my paintbrush down and stepped away from the wall too.

My mother said, "Erica, would you please start gathering up the paint and brushes and putting them in a safe place? Dolores, why don't you and Claudia take the children in small groups to the bathroom to clean them up as much as you can? Miss Ellway and I will keep an eye on everything while you do."

We didn't argue. We did as we were told.

It took awhile, but soon almost everything was back to normal. Fortunately, none of the parents seemed to mind that some of their kids looked like walking rainbows. A few seemed amused.

Ms. Feld, appearing shaken, helped pick up the newspaper from the floor. Erica and I spent most of the rest of the day cleaning up the mess and shelving books.

At the end of the day, Ms. Feld said, "Claudia, could I speak to you for a minute in my office?"

Uh-oh. "Of course," I said.

Erica whispered, "Want me to stick around?"

"No. That's okay." I glanced at my watch. My date with Alan and the entire BSC was approaching. Good grief.

"Good luck," Erica said.

But I didn't need it — at least, not with Ms. Feld. She was smiling again. I don't think anything gets Ms. Feld down for long. She said, "Well, it didn't work out quite the way I'd planned, but I haven't given up on our mural, Claudia. I just wanted you to know that."

"Really?"

"No. We just need to work out a few details."

"Oh." I wondered what kind of details Ms. Feld had in mind. I didn't want to ask.

"Anyway, as soon as we do, we'll get back to work on it," she said.

"Right." I said good-bye to Ms. Feld and dashed out into the hall. If I ran all the way home, I'd have plenty of time to . . .

"Claudia."

My mother's voice. It stopped me in my tracks.

"Mom. Hi. I'm kind of in a hurry."

"This will only take a minute," she said. Her voice was calm — too calm.

She led me into her office, fixed me with a steely look, and said, "Claudia. While I appreciate your creativity, this time you may have gone a little too far."

"Things did get a little out of hand," I admitted. "But Ms. Feld and I will work it out. I promise."

"It's not up to Ms. Feld and you. And I'd appreciate it if, until we decide what to do, you'd just do the job for which you were hired. I understand you are very conscientious and a good worker and I'm proud of you for that. So for the time being, focus on it."

I understood what she was saying: Yo, Claudia — about the art? Thanks but no thanks.

Stiffly, I replied, "I understand. I have to go."

My sense of injustice lent wings to my feet. I got home in record time, bursting through the door of my room like a paint-splattered tornado.

My clock told me that I had fifteen minutes to get ready, fifteen minutes to transform myself from Claudia the human drop cloth to Claudia the work of art.

This was a job for . . . Superclaudia. And since, unlike Superman, I had no phone booth handy, I practically leaped into the closet to begin my transformation.

❀ Chapter 11

Eeek! Not the closet. The bathroom first. I couldn't touch my good clothes with my paint-smeared self. Slamming out of the room with my robe clutched in my least painty hand, I headed for the shower.

Janine was just emerging from her room. "Claudia," she said. "You're covered in paint."

"No kidding. And I have a date in less than fifteen minutes."

"That *will* be a challenge," she said.

"Tell me about it." I dove into the bathroom and went to work on paint removal.

Five minutes later, more or less paint-free, I was tossing clothes around the room as if they were Frisbees.

"No, no, no, yes, maybe . . ." I paused to sniff

something, unsure whether it had fallen off a hanger and was clean or had been dropped on the floor after being worn. "No," I decided, and dropped it back on the closet floor.

Not too dressy. That would look as if I were trying too hard. Or maybe as if I were worried. Not too casual. It was, after all, a date. Something special but basic. Smashing, but understated.

Okay, understated for me.

I settled in the end for beige linen shorts, an enormous red, blue, and purple tie-dyed T-shirt that I had made earlier in the summer, a pair of earrings I'd made from bottle caps and glitter, and purple high-tops with blue socks folded over the top.

I didn't have time to check out the overall effect, because I'd just finished rolling the socks over the high-tops when someone knocked on the door of my room. It was Mary Anne, Stacey, Dawn, and Kristy, on time to the minute.

"We're here," Kristy announced unnecessarily. She looked at her watch, scowled, and said, "Alan's late."

The doorbell rang.

"No, he's not," I replied, sighing inwardly. Was it my imagination, or did Kristy look disappointed?

We hurried downstairs and opened the door. My

group faced Alan's — he'd brought along Cary Retlin and Pete Black.

"Cary," said Kristy. "What are you doing here?"

"I'm glad to see you too," said Cary. At the end of the walk, I could see Mr. Gray in his minivan.

Everyone seemed to step back at the same time, and Alan and I looked at each other. "Let's go," I said, sounding a little like Ms. Feld at her most upbeat.

Side by side, Alan and I walked to the van. Alan held the door for me to get in, and continued to hold it until everyone else was in too.

Then he climbed into the front next to his father.

Mr. Gray said, "We brought the minivan for miniature golf." He guffawed.

Alan gave his father a pained look, which surprised me. I would have expected him to laugh at a joke like that.

"Nice weather for golf," Alan said.

"Have you ever played before, Kristy?" Cary asked.

"Yes," said Kristy, folding her arms. "Why?" Kristy doesn't trust Cary, and with good reason. One never knows when Cary is going to do something outrageous just to "keep life interesting." He's a bit of a mystery man at school, a newcomer who has a number of interesting skills, such as the ability to open locks and to make things vanish, magicianlike, before your eyes. He got Kristy's watch once, right off her wrist, and she never even noticed.

"No reason," said Cary, smiling the smile of the innocent. Involuntarily, I glanced down at my wrist, just to make sure my watch hadn't vanished.

Pete hadn't said anything. Neither had Dawn, Stacey, or Mary Anne. I gave Stacey a Look. She took the hint and said, "What about you, Pete? Do you play golf?"

Pete shrugged. "It's not my sport, but I guess I can handle it."

"I've never played," said Stacey. "At least not real golf. In New York City, they don't have a lot of room for golf courses."

"Golf courses pollute the environment," Dawn said out of the blue, "with all the pesticides and herbicides they use to keep them green."

Somehow, I realized, we were all looking at Alan, as if waiting for him to come out with one of his dumb jokes. At that point, I would have welcomed one, dumb or not.

Alan looked as if he wanted to say something. Then he met my eyes, smiled, and shrugged.

"I think this golf course is kept green by paint, mainly," I said quickly.

To my relief, before the conversation could bog down any further, we turned into the parking lot of the miniature golf course.

So this is my confession: I totally love the Stoneybrook MiniPutt Kingdom. That's what it's called. Whoever designed it didn't stick to any one theme. He or she just let the old imagination out of the cage. As a result, the course looks like a fairy tale crashed into a zoo that also happened to have a couple of dinosaurs and possibly a pirate in it.

I couldn't help smiling. My dad used to take Janine and me to the MiniPutt Kingdom when we were kids. I had a sudden memory of my grandmother Mimi with us, bending over to examine the mouth of the "fire"-breathing dragon as it opened and closed. Beside the dragon's head, which was resting at the end of the putting alley, was a sign that said PLEASE DON'T FEED THE DRAGON! Of course, that was the whole idea — to put the golf ball into the dragon's mouth when it was open. If you succeeded, puffs of smoke came out of its ears and nose.

"*How* have I missed this?" Cary said, sliding out of the car.

"Stoneybrook has many fine features," Pete answered him solemnly.

"I'm going to go hit a bucket of balls over there," Mr. Gray said, pointing to the driving range that flanked the MiniPutt Kingdom.

"Okay," said Alan.

Once again, I found myself standing next to him. I smiled encouragingly at him. "Let's get started," I said, and led the way to the admissions window.

"Let's play pairs," Cary said.

"Fine," said Kristy. "Mary Anne, will you — "

But Cary cut in. "I can ask her myself. Mary Anne, will you do me the honor of being my partner?"

"Sure," said Mary Anne, smiling. She and Cary have had a little bond ever since he helped her with a problem involving a class bully.

Kristy's face reddened. She doesn't like it when someone else takes charge, especially Cary.

He ignored her. "And Pete and Stacey, that's another pair, and Claudia and Dawn, and Kristy and Alan."

What? I gave Cary a Double Nasty Look. Kristy's Look would have melted rock. What was Cary doing?

"But, but, but . . ." Kristy sputtered.

"What's the matter?" Cary asked. "Is something wrong?"

Mary Anne, seeing that Kristy was about to explode, possibly for real, said quickly, "That's settled."

"What?" I said aloud.

I think Dawn was trying not to laugh. "Don't worry, Claudia," she said in a loud voice. "We'll show them that girls rule."

Cary and Mary Anne headed for the first hole, which featured a pirate ship, a plank (down which you putted), and a pirate swinging a cutlass and reciting in a tinny, tape-recorded voice, "Yo-ho-ho, mates! Walk the plank!"

We ended up in groups of four. Somehow, I'm not sure how, Cary maneuvered Dawn and me into his group. Alan, Kristy, Pete, and Stacey followed us in the other.

Since they were behind us, it was very hard to concentrate. I kept looking over my shoulder. Kristy seemed to be ignoring Alan. Pete, I noticed, was focusing most of his attention on Stacey. Alan was playing miniature golf as if his life depended on it.

From time to time, I heard bits of conversation. Like this.

Kristy: Alan, you call that a shot? You weren't even close.

Alan: You're right. Too bad I can't take it over.

Kristy: The face on that dinosaur reminds me of someone. . . . Hmmm . . . Alan! It's you!

Alan: I've never been compared to a dinosaur before.

I heard Mary Anne break into laughter and looked up to discover that we had reached the dragon putt — and that Mary Anne had somehow wedged her golf ball in one of the dragon's nostrils.

"Way to go," Dawn said.

"Thank you, thank you," Mary Anne replied, bowing slightly.

"Your turn, Claudia. Top it if you can," Cary said. I looked up to find him smiling at me. He said more softly, "I think everything is safe in the sandbox right now. Leave them alone and they'll play nicely."

I knew he was referring to Kristy and Alan. And he was right.

I whacked the ball into the dragon's mouth and

took my own bow as smoke poured out of its ears — and one of its nostrils.

We took a break and drank sodas at a picnic table overlooking the course. I watched a little girl wind herself up to hit a bright yellow ball. Unfortunately she kept on winding up until she fell over. It was a Jackie Rodowsky move, and I couldn't help but laugh.

The little girl laughed too, looking at her older sister. Standing up, she tried again — and missed again.

"Good grief," said Kristy.

"She'll get it," said Cary. "She just might have to learn the hard way."

Kristy turned back to narrow her eyes at him. "What is that supposed to mean, exactly?"

"She's stubborn," Alan said. "I admire that."

On her third try, the little girl had made contact with the ball. It dribbled a foot and stopped. This sent her into gales of laughter.

Kristy spun around. "Who's stubborn?" she asked. (Kristy is widely known — and described — as stubborn.)

"The junior golf pro out there," Alan said.

"Oh," said Kristy.

The little girl got it at last. The ball rolled unsteadily through the castle door, and a princess popped out of the tower to wave. The little girl waved back before trotting happily after her sister.

"Well, this *is* fun," Cary said. "Isn't it?"

"This is one thing New York City definitely lacks — and needs more of," Stacey said. "I can see it now: a MiniPutt Kingdom in Times Square, another one in Central Park . . ."

"It's not a bad idea for a park," said Pete seriously.

"It beats actual golf courses," Dawn said. "And I might even like golf courses a little, if they had pirates and princesses on them."

Cary announced, "Claudia's beating Dawn."

"Piece of cake," I said, and Dawn gave me a friendly shoulder punch.

"And I'm beating Mary Anne."

"Not by much," said Mary Anne.

"So what about you guys? Pete, Stacey?"

"She may be a beginner, but she's too good for me — so far," said Pete, grinning at Stacey.

Kristy's lower lip stuck out. She looked amazingly like Claire Pike about to launch into a temper tantrum. I braced myself.

"I'm winning," she said.

"Congratulations!" Cary said.

"You are a very good player," added Alan.

"You're pretty bad," Kristy shot back. "Like you're not even trying."

Alan flushed slightly. He shrugged and gave her an apologetic smile.

Cary had watched it all, a little smile on his face.

I finished my Coke with a noisy slurp. "Come on," I said. "We still have to cross the bridge of the Three Billy Goats Gruff, not to mention getting through Alligator Alley."

Kristy didn't say much the rest of the afternoon. When we returned to my house, I looked at Alan. "Thanks," I said.

"Sure," he replied.

I couldn't say more, not with Pete and especially Cary watching. And although Dawn, Mary Anne, and Stacey had withdrawn to a discreet distance, I could feel Kristy's scowl at my shoulder.

The van had barely pulled away from the curb before Kristy burst out, "Thank goodness *that's* over with! Who knew Alan could be such a wimp!"

❀ Chapter 12

Wimp. A strong word from Kristy. In fact, one of her most derisive labels.

And, I thought uneasily, not the label you'd usually apply to Alan. Alan was anything but a wimp. Furthermore, his behavior at the mini-golf course had definitely not been Alan-as-I-knew-him.

I was thinking about this as Erica and I walked to her house after our day at the library on Thursday. As we'd passed the mutilated mural, I had averted my eyes. It was painful to look at. The topic of the mural had been absent from all my conversations with Ms. Feld that day, from which I had deduced that she had: a) not talked to my mother about it, or b) she had talked to her and was so upset that she didn't want to discuss it with me.

We had stopped by my mom's office. She wasn't there, nor was she at the front desk. Miss Ellway said she was in the staff lounge.

"Would you tell her I'm going over to Erica's house, please?" I'd said.

"Sure," said Miss Ellway.

I was relieved I didn't have to talk to my mother any more than necessary.

"Continuing trouble with the maternal unit?" Erica asked after we'd put some distance between us and the library. I'd been keeping her up to speed, more or less, on my "artistic differences" with Mom.

"Yes. She's blaming me for the mural mess. She thinks I shouldn't have made the suggestion in the first place, among other things." I sighed.

"She'll get over it," said Erica. "Especially when you get the real mural up."

"*If* I ever do. Part of me wants to confront her and part of me wants to lay low. So I'm sort of dithering. And feeling like a wimp."

Wimp. Kristy's word again.

Of course, I'd had something to say to her the night before. We all had. So what if Alan had let her win at miniature golf, as she insisted he had? So what if he had agreed with everything she said? He hadn't made any stupid, gross jokes. He hadn't acted like a clown. He hadn't made Kristy into the butt of his sometimes-less-than-witty wit.

"What more do you want, Kristy?" Stacey had asked. "The guy was on his best behavior. You can't say *that* got on your nerves."

"It did. It was so . . . so . . . fake," she replied.

Stung, I said, "What do you mean, fake?"

"Not normal." Kristy stopped, searching for just the right word. "It just wasn't . . . natural."

"He was very sweet," Mary Anne put in.

Dawn nodded. "He was clearly trying hard to be on his best behavior."

"Well, it was weird," said Kristy. "I can't explain it, but I don't like it."

"I give up!" I said. "Just don't give me any more grief about going out with Alan."

Kristy opened her mouth, then closed it resolutely. I was glad of that. Whatever she was going to say, I didn't want to hear it.

And part of the reason, I now realized, was that I sort of, *kind of* agreed with her. It *wasn't* natural. It *wasn't* Alan. This new, perfectly polite and incredibly self-effacing Alan wasn't real. And wasn't much fun.

Could it be that I missed the old Alan?

"Claudia?" Erica said. "You in there?"

"Sorry." I filled her in on what had been distracting me.

Erica was sympathetic. "Maybe you should talk to Alan," she suggested.

"But what do I say?" I pressed the heel of my hand to my forehead. I felt like tearing out my hair. I'd half-hoped Alan would appear at the library that day. When he hadn't, I hadn't known whether to be disappointed or relieved. "I don't want the old Alan back either."

"It's a problem," said Erica. She lowered her voice and intoned, "*The Two Faces of Alan*."

I sighed — and changed the subject. I was getting good at changing the subject these days. We talked about movies until we reached Erica's house.

She slammed the door behind her and shouted, "HEY! IT'S ME! ANYBODY HOME?"

Nobody answered.

The only sound was of clocks ticking.

"Good," said Erica, relief in her voice. "Come on." She led the way to her bedroom, dumped her books on her bed, and turned to face me. "Remember when you said you'd help me find the names of my birth parents?"

I nodded.

"You meant it?"

"Of course I meant it," I said. "I don't say things I don't mean."

Erica smiled, but she looked tense. "Good," she said. "This is the deal. After all that Web searching and research, I realized that I was wasting my time."

"You're going to talk to your parents again?" I suggested hopefully.

"No! I'm going to do some research right here at home. The day before yesterday I told my mom we should check my passport to see when it expires. She got it out of the little vault in the bedroom closet, and when she did, I saw some papers in there. One of them could be it, Claudia!"

"It?" I was bewildered.

"My birth certificate! With my birth parents' names on it. Anyway, I know the combination for the safe."

I gave Erica a look of awe and respect. I would never have thought of doing something like that.

My respect changed to uneasiness, however, when Erica went on to explain that she wanted *me* to help her open the safe and go through the contents. "You want me to be a . . . safecracker?" I asked.

"We're not breaking into it. I have the combination. No one will ever know," Erica said.

"Your parents will when you suddenly have the

names of your birth parents," I pointed out.

"Maybe I won't tell them. I mean, this is for me. I don't have to tell my parents," Erica argued. "And you said you'd help. I'll open the safe. I just want you to be here, listen for someone coming home. That's all. Please."

I *had* promised. What could I do? "Okay," I said. "Come on, then. Let's get this over with."

"Thanks, Claudia." Erica wasted no time. A minute later we were crouched in her mother's closet, looking at a small gray safe squatting in the back. Erica produced a flashlight from her parents' bedside table, and I held it while she twirled the dial of the safe. I didn't look at the combination — not that I would have remembered the numbers anyway.

The door opened and we both bent forward. Erica lifted out a small box and opened it. Jewelry. She put it back inside, moved an envelope that said LAST WILL AND TESTAMENT and pulled another, larger box forward. Raising the lid, she peered inside.

At that moment, I was sure I heard a car pulling into the driveway. I leaped up and raced to the window, forgetting the flashlight in my hand and leaving Erica in the closet in the dark.

"Hey!" she protested.

"I thought I heard something!" I whispered. But

when I peered around the edge of the curtains, all I saw was an empty driveway.

With a sigh of relief, I joined Erica again. I pointed the flashlight over her shoulder, and she began to sift through the papers in the box. A stack of letters tied with a ribbon would have tempted me, but Erica wasn't interested. She pushed those aside and dug deeper.

And then she froze.

"What?" I said. I straightened. "Did you hear something?"

"No. Claudia, this is it! I've found it! Quick, the flashlight!"

I turned the beam of the flashlight on the piece of paper Erica was holding up in the shadowy closet. It was a birth certificate — for "Baby Girl Stiller."

"It's my birthday. It's me," Erica whispered. I stared and then I looked at the lines beneath "Baby Girl Stiller."

There, spotlighted in the circle of light, were the baby's parents' names. And they weren't the Blumbergs.

They were Alison Stiller and Jonathan Gardener.

❋ Chapter 13

"They're nice names," I said stupidly. I couldn't think of anything else to say. I noticed that the flashlight was shaking a little and clamped my other hand over the one holding the light to make it stay still.

Erica stood up, still holding the box, and walked out of the closet.

"Where are you going?" I asked, alarmed.

"I have to write down the information," she said. She sounded calm. How come *I* was the one who was shaking?

I didn't know what else to do, so I followed Erica back to her room and watched as she took a notebook from a desk drawer, opened it to the middle, and wrote out the information. She closed the notebook (which said MATH PROBLEMS on the front) and returned it to the drawer.

Then she went back to the safe and put the box inside. As the door closed, I breathed a sigh of relief. "Let's get out of here," I said.

We raced down the hall to Erica's room. She closed the door behind us, went back to her desk, took out the notebook, and opened it to the page where she'd written her birth parents' names.

I'd stopped shaking. I took a deep breath.

Erica began to cry. *Really* cry.

"Erica," I said, alarmed. "Erica, it's okay."

She gulped and sobbed, one fist clenched on top of the notebook. "It's them, it's them," she said.

"It is," I agreed, making my voice as soothing as I could.

"I know their names."

"You do." I put my hand over the clenched fist. "You really do."

She sniffed and grabbed a tissue. Then she blew her nose. She wiped her eyes on her shirt sleeve, sniffed once more, and said, almost in a wail, "Claudia! What am I going to do?"

"I don't know," I said. "What do you want to do?"

"I don't knooow." The tears welled up again. I quickly handed her a tissue. She dabbed her eyes and repeated softly, "I don't know."

Poor Erica. She looked so miserable. I wondered

if she'd really believed she'd find her birth certificate, just like that.

I hadn't expected to find it. I don't know what I'd expected.

Then two words floated into my brain.

Be honest.

I looked at Erica. Her head was down.

"Erica," I said. "This is what I think you should do. You should be honest."

"What you do mean?" Erica raised her eyes to meet mine.

"You have to tell your parents what you've found out. You can't keep this a secret. It's too big. You can't handle it alone."

"But if I tell them, and they realize how upset I am, they'll say it proves I was too young to learn my birth parents' names."

"What if it does? It's a done deal."

"It is, isn't it?" Erica said slowly. She squeezed her eyes shut for a moment, then opened them to meet mine again. "Okay. I'll tell them. As soon as they get home."

"Good." I stood up.

Erica went on, "And you'll stay and help me, won't you, Claudia?"

How could I say no?

Mr. and Mrs. Blumberg were *not* happy with the news. Her mother had come home first and knocked on the door of Erica's room. Seeing me, she'd smiled. "Claudia! Are you going to join us for dinner?"

"Uh, I, ah . . ." I stammered. "Uh, not exactly."

"Mom, could I talk to you and Dad? Together? As soon as Dad gets home?" Erica came to my rescue.

Mrs. Blumberg raised an eyebrow. "Of course, honey. Is everything all right?"

"I think so," said Erica. At that moment, Mr. Blumberg called out, "Anybody home?"

"Yes!" Erica said, bouncing to her feet.

"Why don't we go to the kitchen? You can put some hot water on for tea while I get out of these shoes — they're killing my feet — and then your father and I will join you," Mrs. Blumberg said.

"Okay." Erica grabbed my arm and practically yanked me after her.

We made the tea. We sat down. I spent the next twenty minutes gripping the hot mug and never saying a word as Erica told her story.

"Claudia helped because I made her," she concluded. "So please don't blame her."

My face turned red.

Mrs. Blumberg, her expression shocked, said, "I don't blame anybody. But Erica, how could you?"

"I *had* to," Erica said earnestly. "It was driving me crazy."

Mr. Blumberg reached out to rest his hand on his wife's. "It had to happen sooner or later, Rachel. We were going to give her the information eventually."

"But not like this! I wanted to tell you, Erica. To fill in the details . . ." Mrs. Blumberg's voice trailed off.

Tears had sprung up in Erica's eyes. She said, her voice choked, "Mom, I'm sorry. I didn't mean to hurt you."

"Oh, honey, it's not me . . . it's you I'm worried about." Mrs. Blumberg stood up and put her arms around Erica.

Erica turned her face into her mother's shoulder and began to cry in earnest. Maybe Erica really wasn't ready for this just yet.

"I guess we need to decide where to go from here," said Mr. Blumberg, almost to himself.

"Speaking of going," I said, "I've got to get home."

I don't think Mrs. Blumberg or Erica heard me. Mr. Blumberg nodded. He gave me a lopsided smile.

" 'Bye," I said, and made my escape.

It had been a long, hard day. And I had a feeling that for Erica, finding out what she'd wanted to know wasn't going to make things easier. At least not right away.

❋ Chapter 14

"You're late," were the first words my mother said to me as I walked through the kitchen door.

"I was at Erica's," I answered vaguely. Being a part of what had happened at Erica's house had made me feel like a painting composed of wild drips and dabs. "I left a message for you."

"I got the message. But you're still late."

I sat down limply at the kitchen table where Mimi and I had sat so many times, drinking tea and hot chocolate. I had talked to Mimi. I had been honest with her. Nothing was too trivial or strange for me to tell her. I knew she would never, ever stop loving me.

Just as Erica had to know that her parents would never, ever stop loving her. They might not always understand her, but they would always love her.

That was why it was so important to be honest with the people you loved — the people who loved you.

I looked up at Mom. She hadn't moved, and I realized that she wasn't angry so much as worried and a little puzzled. She said, "Claudia?"

And I said, "Oh, Mom!" and jumped up to hug her.

She was startled, but she hugged me back. She didn't say anything. I leaned against her and smelled her familiar Mom-smell of perfume and powder and shampoo, and yes, books. I hugged her harder.

She said, "Claudia, it'll be all right, whatever it is."

And I said, "I'm an artist, Mom. I didn't think about who to ask for permission or who was the boss. I just thought about how to make the wall look beautiful, and I wanted you to be proud of me."

"Oh, Claudia." Now my mother's arms tightened around me. "I *am* proud of you. Every day in every way. Don't you know that?"

"No. Yes. Maybe."

She let go and stepped back. "I know you see the world differently, and I wish I could see it a little more the way you do. I imagine it's a wonderful world."

"Sometimes," I said. "And sometimes I can't make sense of anything I see. That's why I like art so much, I guess. If I can just put down what I see, the way I see it, then I can figure out what I'm looking at."

It didn't make much sense, but *I* knew what I was talking about. My mother smiled. "Words do it for me," she said. "I always wished I could write, but I'm not much good at it. That's why I love reading. I look for writers who can write down what I feel. If I can find that, then I can make sense out of the world."

I'd never thought about words or writing in quite that way. I'd never known my mother wanted to be a writer. All I could think to say was, "Wow."

A deeply dumb thing to say. But my mother laughed aloud. "The perfect word," she said. "Exactly. Wow."

Then I laughed too. I heard footsteps in the hall and knew it was my father. It was time to get ready for dinner.

I said quickly, "Don't worry about the mural. I can fix it. That is, if you'll trust me. On my own, not on library time."

"I trust you," said my mom. "And if Ms. Feld wants you to work on it as part of your job, that's between you and Ms. Feld." She paused and said, "Although I'm not sure about that group effort . . ."

"I'll find a way for the kids to be part of the mural without making a total mess," I promised. "In fact, I already have an idea."

"Next," I said, a few days later.

Erica led four children out into the hall, which was once again lined with old newspapers. I looked at the four children who'd just finished "working" on the mural. They held out their paint-sticky hands carefully.

Erica handed me a stack of clothing — old work shirts and aprons that I'd brought from home. As she led the four artists to the bathroom to get cleaned up, she said, "Don't touch *anything*."

My new group of artists included Jackie Rodowsky. I chose the biggest shirt for him and swaddled him in it. Then I put aprons or shirts in more matching sizes on the other three.

I led them to the wall. The bottom and sides had been painted over with quick-drying paint to make a border. Now handprints and names were filling in that border. One at a time, I let each artist dip a palm into one of the shallow tin pans of color I'd arranged on the floor. Jackie went first. He put a bright red, slightly smeared handprint near the corner of the mural. Then, with my help, he signed his first name beneath it.

"Excellent," I said. "You're now officially part of the Stoneybrook Library mural. And you can wave at yourself every time you walk by."

Jackie grinned. "That's silly," he said.

"That's art," I replied — which was a silly thing to say too. But Jackie didn't mind. He stepped carefully back and watched as the others added their handprints and names.

Four by four, every child in the story session put his or her handprint and name on the border of the mural. We'd do this for the next couple of weeks, to make sure all the kids would be included. I'd also made signs and put them at the front desk and at the children's room desk: "Kids! Be an Artist for the Stoneybrook Library. Ask Ms. Feld in the Children's Room to Give You a Hand!"

Yes, I made that awful pun. Alan had been rubbing off on me, clearly. But it was a pretty good joke. My mom grinned when she saw it and shook her head.

Alan. He wasn't quite in focus on the muddled

canvas that was my mind. But the picture was getting clearer. Definitely.

After story hour, Erica talked to me while she ate her lunch and I worked. I'd painted out the sections that were to be removed and was sketching in the new figures.

"What's happening at your house?" I asked as I painted in the castle tower where Rapunzel read her book and let down her long golden hair.

"We talked. And talked." Erica sighed. "I'm tired. And relieved."

"You must be," I said, thinking of how much better I felt since I'd talked with my mom.

"Totally. But you know what's funny? My parents said I could go ahead with my search — and now I'm not even sure I want to."

"Mmm," I said neutrally. Then I added, "It's sort of like a mystery. You know, solving it is what matters, and then once you've figured it out, it's not so . . ."

"Compelling." Erica supplied the word for me. "That's right. I was obsessed with the search. And I think I wanted to show my parents I could pull it off. But now, part of me thinks maybe they *were* right. I mean, I'm not all that eager to take the next step. I think, just for now, I'll wait."

"Well, whatever you decide to do, I'll help you if I can," I said.

"Thanks, Claudia. You're a true friend."

"And don't forget 'great artist.' "

"That too," Erica agreed.

I couldn't spend the entire day working on the mural. I still had my regular work to do. But I planned on coming early and staying late to get it just the way I wanted. I wouldn't rush. I would do it right. After all, I had the rest of the summer.

I was still hard at work late that afternoon when Alan showed up.

"Alan," I said. I was really glad to see him.

"Hey, Claudia." He sounded *reasonably* happy to see me. But he was not his usual exuberant self.

"Did you come to give me a hand?" I asked. I gestured at the row of handprints that were scattered along the borders of the mural.

Alan smiled. "Good one. And the mural looks like it has potential."

"Oh, it does. Believe me."

"The artist is always right?"

"You know she is," I answered. I stopped. I was giving Alan a chance to make one of his corny jokes. But he didn't. He just looked at me, then at the mural, as if he couldn't quite meet my eyes. I noticed then that he had folded his arms in front of him. He did not look comfortable.

And I didn't feel comfortable with this other side of Alan.

"Hey," I said. "Let me get things cleaned up here, and then I'll show you my favorite place in the library." I waved my hand around. "Meanwhile, maybe you can find a book to read while you wait."

Alan smiled. Politely. "Okay," he said.

"Okay," I said.

"What is this, a dungeon?" Alan asked.

"Nope." I led the way down a narrow flight of stairs at the back of one of the book storage closets in the reference corner of the main library. I pushed open the door at the bottom. The floor there was made of uneven bricks. Two steps brought me to a brick wall with a door just to the right of it. I pushed that door open, and we were in a small square room made of bricks. A dehumidifer hummed in the corner, but other than that, the room was quiet. Bookshelves covered most of the walls, but in places you could see the fan pattern in which the bricks had been laid, which echoed the pattern beneath our feet.

"It *is* a dungeon," Alan said.

I shook my head. "Have a box," I said, indicating one of the storage boxes on the floor. I sat down.

Alan sat down facing me. "It's part of the original building that was here," I explained. "It was an old farmhouse, I think. Nothing big or fancy, but the man who built the house was a mason, and he put a lot of work into it. He made the bricks himself, by hand. That's why they're uneven and different colors." I ran my hand over the rough surface of the nearby wall. I wish I could paint textures like that.

"How do you know all that?" Alan asked.

I shrugged. "Mom told me. The library uses this space now to store things that Mom doesn't quite know what to do with but doesn't want to throw away. Right now, it's mostly the old card catalog files." I gestured at the card-sized file boxes lining the bookshelves. "Some of the files are really old, written by hand. Librarians had to learn a special kind of writing for the files, so they could be sure that people could read them."

"If I had a job like that, I'd make up some cool books that should be written and put them in the files," Alan said. "I'd . . ." He stopped.

"What?" I asked.

"Nothing."

"Alan," I said. "Stop it."

"Stop what?" He looked alarmed and very defensive. "I wasn't doing anything. I've been . . . really careful."

"I know," I said. "And I appreciate it. I mean, that you didn't let Kristy get to you when we played miniature golf and all that. But you don't have to make yourself into some kind of pretzel, holding back when you want to talk. To be yourself."

"Great," said Alan. "A pretzel. So I'm a jerk if I'm myself and I'm a pretzel if I'm not. I'd call that a lose-lose situation."

"Just be yourself," I said.

"I can't!" Alan shot back fiercely. "I'm afraid to!"

I was shocked. "Afraid?"

"You won't like me if I'm myself. Your friends won't like me. I mean, I saw Kristy that day. She was just *waiting* for me to be Alan the clown. The Alan she *hates*. The Alan you don't like either."

"Alan!" I said.

"It's true. Think about it. I sure have."

"Oh, no," I said. "Oh, Alan. Kristy doesn't hate you. She's just having a problem changing the picture she has of you."

"And she won't change it if I start goofing."

"That's not true. Kristy's stubborn, but she's not unfair. *I'm* the one who has been unfair."

"What do you mean?"

"Letting you think I want you to be somebody you're not. But I don't want you to be some perfect, polite, dull robot Alan."

"Dull?" said Alan, looking indignant.

I rushed on. "I've seen the side of you who doesn't cut up and make jokes to answer every question, who doesn't have to be the center of attention, even if that just means everybody's rolling their eyes and shaking their heads. I know a different side of you. But I also like the side of you that does unexpected things, that isn't afraid to see what's funny and go for it."

"Yeah?" Alan thought for a minute. Then he said, "But if I try to be myself — both myselves — what if you don't like that? I mean, I'm not even sure exactly who that Alan is."

I thought about all the ways people tried to find themselves, whether it was searching for birth parents or reading books or making art. It was never ending. You'd get one answer and see another question. I said slowly, "I guess figuring out who you are takes time. Maybe it takes your whole life."

"You're not sure yet?" Alan asked.

I looked up. Alan was grinning.

"Not yet. But I'm working on it. And I know one thing about me. I've learned that being honest is really important to me. So I'll like you no matter what, as long as you're honest."

Alan put one hand over his heart and raised the other. "I promise to tell the truth, the whole truth, and nothing but the truth."

Then he reached out and caught my hand. "Now, when is my next date with the Baby-sitters Club?"

❁ Chapter 15

"Put the bowls of potato salad at each end of the table so the tablecloth doesn't blow away," Kristy ordered. "And don't forget to cover the food, or you'll have flies all over it."

"Yes, ma'am," said Cary Retlin. He gave an exaggerated bow, hoisted one of the two huge bowls of potato salad from our kitchen counter, and headed out the door to the backyard.

Alan grabbed a flyswatter from a hook on the wall by the door and said, "I'll stand guard over the food."

Kristy rolled her eyes. But she said, "You don't get off that easily, Alan. Fill those glasses with ice and set them out on the table."

Just then, Stacey came into the kitchen and

grabbed two more bottles of soda. "We're almost ready," she said.

Kristy waved an impatient hand. "Salt, pepper? Mustard, ketchup?" she barked, one eye on the oven.

I took pity on her. "I'll watch the cookies, Kristy. I can load some stuff into the dishwasher while I do it. You go make sure everything is running smoothly."

"Okay," said Kristy, and charged out of the kitchen after Dawn.

We were having a Saturday picnic in my backyard: Alan, Kristy, Dawn, Mallory, Jessi, Stacey, Abby, Mary Anne, Cary, Pete, and Erica. Kristy's brother Charlie, who'd given Kristy, Abby, and the potato salad a ride to my house, had also decided to hang around and had somehow made himself chef in charge of the gas grill. Wrapped in an apron, he was tending hot dogs, veggie burgers, and buns as they cooked. I wouldn't be surprised if some of the neighborhood kids didn't find their way to the food and festivities before it was over.

It was a party. It was a celebration. I'd gone whole artistic hog: streamers, balloons in the trees, a "found-art" centerpiece made of pinecones, leaves, flowers, and an assortment of costume jewelry. We'd all brought our favorite food. Dawn and Mary Anne were busy putting the finishing touches on home-made ice cream, and Alan and I had made M&M cookies.

I slipped the cookies out of the oven. I heard Kristy say, "Abby, Jessi, stop playing soccer and come help set the table."

Alan grinned. "She's bossy."

"Organized," I corrected him, smiling back. "She prefers 'organized.'" I pulled the cookies out of the oven.

Alan cleared a space on the table and put down a trivet so I could set the cookie sheet on it.

"Thanks," I said.

"Nothing any organized person wouldn't have done."

"Chips," Pete called through the door. Without pausing, Alan scooped up a bag of chips and said, "Go long!"

He fired the chips through the doorway as if they were a football.

"Touchdown!" Alan shouted, and then I heard a shriek and a crash. Pete had collided with Mary Anne and a bowl of dill pickles. Both of them were now wearing pickles, and Pete had fallen on the bag of chips.

"Who threw those chips?" I heard Kristy shout.

"Could I tell just a little lie now?" Alan asked me.

"No," I said, trying not to laugh.

Alan went to the door, fell to his knees, and threw out his arms. "It was me," he said. "I cannot tell a lie. I put Mary Anne and Pete into this pickle."

Abby laughed, and I saw Cary shake his head and grin. Pete rolled off the bag of chips and held it up. "Good-bye, Mr. Chips," he said.

Abby laughed harder.

Kristy rolled her eyes. Then she said to Alan, "On your feet. This is your punishment. You have to pick up all the pickles. And then you have to say, 'If Alan Gray picked a peck of pickled peppers, how many pecks of pickled peppers did Alan Gray pick?' three times very fast before you can have dessert."

"Yes, ma'am," said Alan, jumping to his feet.

"Come on," Mary Anne said to Pete, "let's go wash off the pickle juice."

Alan turned to me. I rolled my eyes. "You're too much," I said.

"As long as I'm not too much for you," he answered, sounding anxious and hopeful.

"No," I replied, touched.

"Good." He smiled. It wasn't a goofy grin. It was

a sort of special smile, one that he seemed to have saved for me. Then he said, "I like going out with the BSC. Really I do. But I guess I'd like to think of just *you* as my, uh, girlfriend."

I gulped. Possibly I blushed. Then I said, "Okay, boyfriend."

Alan's smile was huge and wonderful.

I smiled back. "Better go pick that peck of pickled peppers," I said.

We had a grand picnic, flies, pickle juice, smashed potato chips, and all. As Mary Anne and Dawn dished out ice cream at the end and I stuck cookies in each bowl, I looked up and down the two picnic tables we'd put together and felt happy to my toes.

Alan, who was sitting next to me, stood up after he'd been served his dish of ice cream. "Attention," he said.

Then he recited the pickled-pepper tongue twister three times.

Perfectly.

When he had finished, he bowed, reached down and grabbed my hand, and raised it in his.

The table broke into cheers and applause. My face turned red, but I didn't let go of Alan's hand.

Whatever happened, Alan and I and all my friends were in it together.

And whatever happened, with Alan Gray around, it was bound to be pretty amazingly interesting.

Ann M. Martin

About the Author

ANN MATTHEWS MARTIN was born on August 12, 1955. She grew up in Princeton, NJ, with her parents and her younger sister, Jane.

Although Ann used to be a teacher and then an editor of children's books, she's now a full-time writer. She gets ideas for her books from many different places. Some are based on personal experiences. Others are based on childhood memories and feelings. Many are written about contemporary problems or events.

All of Ann's characters, even the members of the Baby-sitters Club, are made up. (So is Stoneybrook.) But many of her characters are based on real people. Sometimes Ann names her characters after people she knows; other times she chooses names she likes.

In addition to the Baby-sitters Club books, Ann Martin has written many other books for children. Her favorite is *Ten Kids, No Pets* because she loves big families and she loves animals. Her favorite BSC book is *Kristy's Big Day*. (Kristy is her favorite baby-sitter.)

Ann M. Martin now lives in New York with her cats, Gussie, Woody, and Willy, and her dog, Sadie. Her hobbies are reading, sewing, and needlework — especially making clothes for children.

Look for

GRADUATION DAY

Can't believe am about to graduate. Definitely not ready for it. Possible to graduate from 8th grade, then return to SMS and have a do-over? Am REALLY not ready for high school. Tried to explain this to Mom. Was told am being silly. According to Mom, all freshmen are nervous about starting high school. Since when does Mom consider her dear daughter like everyone else?

Walked through the halls of SMS today and was BOMBARDED by notices about caps and gowns, yearbooks, and like. Every notice frightening. How am I supposed to concentrate on finals with all these distractions? Oh! Maybe if flunk finals will have to repeat 8th grade. Good idea.

Note to self: Ask Charlie if he felt like this when he was leaving SMS. . . .

It was a very hot night — hot for May, that is — and I was lying in my bedroom with the windows open, listening to the late spring nighttime sounds. I'm pretty sure I was the only one in my whole house who was still awake. And with a family my size, that is saying a lot. All around me were bedrooms with sleeping people in them. My mom and Watson in one. (Watson is my stepfather — he's pretty cool, even if he is going bald.) My big brother Charlie in one; my other big brother, Sam, in one; my little brother David Michael in one; my little sister Karen in one; my little brother Andrew in one; my little sister Emily Michelle in one; and my grandmother Nannie in one. And all of them asleep, as far as I knew.

Just me awake and stewing. For three years my friends and I have been edging our way through SMS, or Stoneybrook Middle School. And now, after three years of projects, tests, report cards, field trips, cafeteria meals, softball games, and dances, it's about to end. We are about to graduate and go on to SHS, Stoneybrook High School.

Check out what's new
with your old friends.